"Those are our only options?"

She scoffed. "Unless you can think of something else to do."

Actually, Mac could. Not, he reminded himself sternly, that making an ill-conceived pass at her was one of the options....

This was a business situation. Or at least it had been, until they had started sharing personal stories and whiling away the time together.

Then it had become something else. Something a lot more treacherous...and interesting.

Erin groaned and let out a nervous laugh. "Forget I said that."

The gentlemanly side of Mac knew he should. Only trouble was, he wasn't feeling particularly chivalrous right now. He was feeling...turned on. And she was, too, otherwise her mind wouldn't have gone in the exact same direction his had.

The direction that would land them in each other's arms.

At least for a kiss.

"Actually," Mac said casually, turning toward her, and taking her slender body into his arms. Going on instinct, he slowly lowered his head. "I don't think I will."

Dear Reader,

We all have plans for our lives, formed as we grow up. I thought I was going to live in a house with a white picket fence. (Didn't happen, although I do have a fence, and I do have a house.) I thought I'd marry a great guy (did happen), a brilliant absent-minded professor type (he is that) who also could make me laugh like no one else. (Gotta admit, he can be hilarious.) I also figured I'd be a mom and have a career, and that all took place, too.

But what ensues, I wondered, when the plans you've made take detours that aren't the kind that are easily recovered from?

Mac Wheeler grew up wanting a high-powered career and a wife and family, and he had all that—until the day an unexpected tragedy occurred, and he found himself a single dad with a traveling lifestyle that was not right for his only child.

Erin Monroe loved her life, but suddenly found herself the family matriarch at age 23, raising her brothers and sisters, and eventually her own brood. Then life sent her into another tailspin—one that left her functioning, but emotionally numb, just going through the motions of life.

The day Erin and Mac come face-to-face, neither believe they will ever love again. But as they say, life has a way of happening when you are busy making other plans....

I hope you enjoy this final book of the Legends of Laramie County miniseries. Please visit my website at www.cathygillenthacker.com, and my Facebook and Twitter pages.

Cheers,

Cathy Gillen Thacker

The Texas Rancher's Family

Cathy Gillen Thacker

HARLEQUIN® AMERICAN ROMANCE®

ISBN-13: 978-0-373-75441-0

THE TEXAS RANCHER'S FAMILY

This edition published by arrangement with Harlequin Books S.A.

For questions and comments about the quality of this book, please contact us at CustomerService@Harlequin.com.

Printed in U.S.A.

ABOUT THE AUTHOR

Cathy Gillen Thacker is married and a mother of three. She and her husband spent eighteen years in Texas and now reside in North Carolina. Her mysteries, romantic comedies and heartwarming family stories have made numerous appearances on bestseller lists, but her best reward, she says, is knowing one of her books made someone's day a little brighter. A popular Harlequin Books author for many years, she loves telling passionate stories with happy endings, and thinks nothing beats a good romance and a hot cup of tea! You can visit Cathy's website at www.cathygillenthacker.com for more information on her upcoming and previously published books, recipes and a list of her favorite things.

Books by Cathy Gillen Thacker

HARLEQUIN AMERICAN ROMANCE

1080—THE ULTIMATE TEXAS BACHELOR*
1096—SANTA'S TEXAS LULLABY*
1112—A TEXAS WEDDING VOW*
1125—BLAME IT ON TEXAS *
1141—A LARAMIE, TEXAS CHRISTMAS *
1157—FROM TEXAS, WITH LOVE*
1169—THE RANCHER NEXT DOOR**
1181—THE RANCHER'S FAMILY THANKSGIVING**
1189—THE RANCHER'S CHRISTMAS BABY**
1201—THE GENTLEMAN RANCHER**
1218—HANNAH'S BABY‡
1231—THE INHERITED TWINS‡
1237—A BABY IN THE BUNKHOUSE‡
1254—FOUND: ONE BABY‡
1262—MOMMY FOR HIRE
1278—A BABY FOR MOMMY‡‡
1286—A MOMMY FOR CHRISTMAS‡‡
1298—WANTED: ONE MOMMY‡‡
1319—THE MOMMY PROPOSAL‡‡
1325—THE TRIPLETS' FIRST THANKSGIVING
1334—A COWBOY UNDER THE MISTLETOE†
1350—ONE WILD COWBOY†
1363—HER COWBOY DADDY†
1374—A COWBOY TO MARRY†
1394—THE RELUCTANT TEXAS RANCHER††
1412—THE TEXAS RANCHER'S VOW††
1428—THE TEXAS RANCHER'S MARRIAGE††

*The McCabes: Next Generation
**Texas Legacies: The Carrigans
‡Made in Texas
‡‡The Lone Star Dads Club
†Texas Legacies: The McCabes
††Legends of Laramie County

Chapter One

Erin Monroe sized up her big, strapping customer with a frustrated sigh. What was it about the Philadelphia-based Mac Wheeler that had all the women in Laramie County tripping over themselves to get a moment of his time? Was it his ruggedly handsome face? Dark hair? Breath-takingly sexy blue eyes? The fact the thirtysomething executive exuded confidence and determination? Or the easy masculine grace with which he carried himself?

All she knew for certain was that every time he came to Laramie County to try and drum up support for his solution to the county's electrical energy shortage, he created quite a stir.

And now he had his sights on her. Or on what she could do for him.

Fortunately for both of them, she wasn't about to sell the ambitious exec anything he didn't need and would probably never use.

With as much kindness as she could muster, Erin informed him, "Contrary to what my competitors would likely tell you, Mr. Wheeler, boots do not make the man. Even here in ranch country."

Mac Wheeler lounged against the checkout counter and drawled, "Now, that's an odd thing to say, given the fact you're one of the premier custom boot makers in Texas."

"But in your case it's true." Determined to be honest with him, Erin continued, "New footwear, custom or otherwise, is not going to help you close the deal on the proposed wind farm." There was too much opposition to it. Plus he had nowhere to situate the three hundred forty-two ridiculously huge and intrusive wind turbines he was proposing.

So there was no reason for him to be spending several thousand dollars on a pair of boots. Even if the sophisticated business clothing he wore now indicated he could well afford it.

Mac lifted a brow in surprise. Thus far, people had been politely listening to his suggestions. Even as they privately pooh-poohed his venture.

"This is oil and gas country," Erin explained. "Ranchers don't want miles of power-generating windmills scaring their cattle and horses, and cluttering up the landscape."

Mac straightened to his full height, thoroughly dwarfing her own five-foot-six-inch frame. "They'll change their minds once I have a chance to present my proposal to the Laramie County commissioners later this month." His voice dropped a persuasive notch. "And when I do that, I'll need to fit in."

Erin picked up a stack of new shirts and carried them over to the shelves in the center of the hundred-year-old clothing store, Monroe's Western Wear. Her skin tingled as he fell into step behind her. She wished Mac didn't smell so invigoratingly good, so woodsy and male.

"I understand wanting to connect with the people here, Mr. Wheeler." It was only natural. No one wanted to feel like an outsider. She turned to look him in the eye, and felt another disturbing jolt of awareness. "But dressing as what would likely be perceived as a 'drugstore cowboy' is not going to accomplish that for you."

If anything, it would make his discomfort with the locals worse.

Mac's brows knitted together in consternation. "I thought Monroe's sold only authentic Western wear."

"That's true." Their business sold everything a roper, wrangler or rider needed.

His curious glance took in the floor-to-ceiling shelves of denim that lined the entire back wall. "Then how could I wear anything you sell and not look like a genuine Texan?"

Aware that several ladies shopping nearby were listening intently, Erin propped her hands on her hips and looked him up and down. "You *really* want me to answer that?"

Sheer male confidence radiated from him as he stepped closer. "I wouldn't be here if I didn't," he retorted in the same low, droll tone.

Erin ignored the heat emanating from his tall, muscular frame. "Look—" she stepped back, until her spine came in contact with the nearby shelving "—I could put you in a pair of Wrangler jeans—"

Mac's confused frown deepened. "Don't you mean Levi's?"

What a gringo! Erin shook her head at his ignorance, explaining, "Wranglers have the heavier rolled seam on the outside of the legs. Levi's puts it on the inside. If you're a real cowboy and you're sitting in the saddle, you want the heavier seam where it's not likely to rub."

He seemed momentarily taken aback, apparently realizing that on his own he was likely to end up outfitted like a dude from the city instead of the real thing. "Oh."

Erin lifted a staying hand. "Not that I expect you to be in the saddle anytime soon," she quipped.

Amusement glimmered in his eyes. "You don't think I can ride?"

Could he? Erin tilted her head. He was fit and athletic. Broad-shouldered and powerful-looking, with big, capable hands. In fact, now that she thought about it, if he lost the ultra-sophisticated wool suit, starched shirt and tie, and traded in the wing tips for boots, he would look like he belonged out on the range, instead of behind a desk.

But he wasn't wearing jeans now.

And he hadn't been—from all reports—on his first two trips to town, either.

Whether he knew it or not, that sort of sealed his fate.

The local constituency had decided who—and what—he was. And that meant they wouldn't trust him to solve their highly problematic shortage of electricity.

"No," Erin said finally, aware that he was still waiting for her response. "Although you're a heck of a determined businessperson, I don't think you can ride a horse."

A slow smile tugged at the corners of his lips. "You might be wrong about that," he taunted softly.

Aware that she hadn't been so captivated by a man in ages, Erin widened her eyes. "Am I, now?" she goaded right back.

His grin widened. "You'd have to agree to make me a pair of custom boots to find out."

"As I told you on the phone earlier, you're going to need to make an appointment for that."

He nodded, repeating dutifully, "And the first appointment is in six months."

"Correct. But if you like," Erin conceded, "my brother, Nicholas, could sell you off-the-rack whatever you think you need, including a pair of ready-made boots."

Nicholas waved from behind the counter. Mac acknowledged the sixteen-year-old with a genial nod, then turned back to her. "But you don't recommend I start dressing like a West Texan, do you?"

She wouldn't lie. "If there's one thing the residents of Laramie County want," she advised kindly, "it's a person to be genuine. They won't see anything honorable in pretending to be something you're not."

Mac rubbed his closely shaved jaw and peered at her. "So you really think I'd be better off talking to people as a misplaced Yankee in a suit?"

Erin stood her ground. "Don't you?"

A contemplative silence fell between them.

"As I'm sure you've heard, that hasn't been working so far," Mac said ruefully.

People had been polite, Erin knew, but not at all on board with what he was trying to sell.

She squinted. "So your plan is…"

He shrugged. "To do what I always do and try and 'speak the language' of whatever region I find myself in. And right now, experience tells me I won't ever be successful around here unless I can 'speak Texan.'"

One of the eavesdropping customers hurried on over. "Then you'll be needing one of these." She placed a Texas dictionary in his hand. The semihumorous tome was filled with Lone Star State vernacular.

"Thanks." Mac smiled.

"Maybe a hat," another woman said eagerly, joining the conversation.

Her shopping buddy agreed. "Something dressy that would go with a suit."

Erin tried to picture Mac in a Stetson or Resistol, and realized he would be sexy as all get-out in either.

"You can wear boots with a suit, too," another shopper pointed out.

Mac turned back to Erin. Smiled. Suddenly, at least a few of the locals were on his side. Of course, Erin noted a little irritably, they were all *female.* And single, at that.

"Or you could pay triple, and get an appointment for custom boots right away, like that country-and-western star who came in last month," Nicholas interjected as he stepped out from behind the counter.

At that, it was all Erin could do not to groan.

Her brother extended his hand to Mac and they shook. "By the way, I'm head of the environmental club at Laramie High School. We've all heard about what you're doing here…and it sure would be great if we could get you to come and speak about wind farms."

"I'll check my calendar and see what I can do," Mac promised.

A chime sounded as the front door opened, and Erin's two sons walked in from school.

As usual, eight-year-old Sammy's clothes were smudged with dirt. A fifth grader, ten-year-old Stevie was much more together.

"Hey, Mom!" they said in unison, stopping to give her a hug before circling around her to drop their backpacks on the shelf behind the sales counter.

Mac smiled at her boys with surprising warmth.

Surprised, because she hadn't figured the sexy bachelor would want much to do with kids, Erin made introductions. The boys shook hands obediently, then took off to get a snack from the fridge in the break room.

Mac turned back to Erin, his expression resolute. "About that appointment… How about five tomorrow evening?"

"It'll take at least two hours," Erin hedged, "and the store closes at six."

"So we'll make it four o'clock," Nicholas interjected practically.

Erin's jaw dropped. Since when did her brother schedule things for her?

He shrugged at her look.

The tall interloper beamed. "I'd sure appreciate that."

Erin gave up arguing about it. "It is going to cost you triple for a rush job," she warned. "Which means the price would likely be closer to twelve thousand dollars for a pair of boots, if you want them by June first."

So if that seemed utterly ridiculous to him...

To her frustration, it didn't.

"No problem," Mac said as he plucked his phone out of his suit jacket, checking the screen. "Sorry. I have to take this," he murmured, then stepped outside into the May sunshine.

"A LITTLE HARD ON HIM, weren't you, sis?" Nicholas asked, the moment Mac Wheeler was out of earshot.

Erin knew she hadn't been as warm and welcoming as she normally would have been to a customer. Maybe because she was way too attracted to the sexy businessman. And these days, with all she had on her shoulders, lust was the last thing she needed to feel. "It annoys me when people insist on jumping line. I think they should wait their turn like everyone else, no matter how much of a hurry they're in." She slipped behind the counter, where another box of merchandise waited to be opened.

"That's not the way the world works," Nicholas countered as he moved to help her unpack it. "Besides, it's not like we don't need the money. With the electricity rates and the property taxes on the ranch both going sky-high, Bess and Bridget still in college, and me about to go next…"

Their budget was stretched to the limit, despite the store's continued success.

The door opened. Mac Wheeler strode back in, sunglasses on. The set of his mouth was as tense as his shoulders. "I'm going to have to head East."

Erin nodded, not the least bit surprised to see him running off again. Wasn't that the pattern of all the men she was attracted to? Here one moment, gone the next?

He consulted the calendar on his phone. "I'll be back the day after tomorrow. So if we could move the appointment to Wednesday afternoon at four?"

He'd been a customer less than ten minutes and was already demanding more special treatment, Erin noted irritably.

Her little brother regarded Mac with hero worship. "No problem. We're here whenever you need us."

"I appreciate that." Mac touched an index finger to his forehead in a salute. "Nicholas, Ms. Monroe, I'll see you then."

MAC GOT IN LATE and promptly took care of the personal situation that had summoned him home. Midmorning the following day, he stopped by corporate headquarters in downtown Philadelphia, to give his boss an update.

Louise Steyn motioned him into her office and shut the door behind them. Elegant as always in a tailored designer suit, she slipped behind her desk. "When do you think you'll have this deal wrapped up?"

Mac settled in a chair opposite her. "Another month, maybe two."

"What's the holdup?" she asked.

How could he explain that even their company's

name—North Wind Energy—was offensive to the prickly Texans? "It's complicated."

"Laramie County should be jumping at the chance to lower their electric rates."

Maybe they would be if it had been a community comprised mostly of suburban homes, and the size of their electric bills was the only quandary, Mac reasoned. "There are a lot of ranches. The residents are very attached to the land, and how each property looks."

Louise shrugged. "They'll like clean, plentiful, renewable energy even more."

"I'm on it," he promised. All he needed was a decent forum to make his pitch, and a place to situate the wind farm. He had the first and was close to getting the other.

Louise paused to look him in the eye. "Everything okay at home? I heard there was some kind of crisis that brought you back to Philly last night."

Mac thought about the tears—from both females—that had greeted his arrival. "I'm handling it."

Louise gave him the same look she'd given him two and a half years before. "If there's anything you need in that respect…" she volunteered.

He ignored the tinge of pity in her manner. Life went on. The difficulty he was navigating was only temporary. "Thanks," he said quietly, rising from his chair. "I'll keep that in mind." The meeting over, he turned and headed out.

Selling a project he could handle. Dealing with the domestic drama on the home front? He could manage that, too, with a few temporary adjustments. It was the pretty owner of Monroe's Western Wear who was a thorn in his side.

Mac knew she was one of the most respected businesspeople in town. Heck, if you considered the reputation of the boots Erin Monroe made, in the entire state. People listened to her. And not just because she was smart and savvy, warm and hospitable. Or had an enticing figure, honey-blond curls and big green eyes.

They paid attention to her because she was a natural leader. The kind of person who could make something take place. Or not.

If she was as against the wind farm as she had appeared in their brief conversation, he was going to have a tough time bringing North Wind Energy's biggest project yet to fruition.

But that had to happen—and fast—because making it a reality was the only way he was going to be able to get his home life under control, once and for all.

Chapter Two

Erin was in her second-floor studio, putting the finishing touches on a pair of custom boots to be picked up later that afternoon, when Darcy Purcell, her best friend, part-time employee—and next customer—stuck her head in. "He's back. And he's not alone."

Erin didn't even need to ask who "he" was. Mac Wheeler had been the source of endless speculation in the two days he had been gone. Partly because he had left town so suddenly that he'd had to cancel half a dozen appointments with landowners. The rest, because he had managed to talk her into allowing him to skip the line and get fitted for a pair of custom boots at triple the asking price. That action alone had cemented his reputation with the locals as a foolhardy Yankee.

After all, no one in Laramie wasted money, if they could help it.

Erin wrapped the boots in tissue paper and put them in a box emblazoned with the customer's name. "I could care less," she said, pushing aside the memory of the attractive interloper.

Darcy followed Erin downstairs to the cash register. "Don't you want to know what I heard?"

"No." Erin set the boots beneath the counter, then frowned as a sleek black limo with tinted windows pulled up at the curb. The rear door on the driver's side opened and Mac emerged. His strides long and lazy, he circled around the back of the vehicle, then walked into the rustic interior of her family's store.

If anything, with his dark hair rumpled and his blue eyes intent, he was more devastatingly handsome than ever. Wearing khaki slacks, a button-up shirt and loafers, he still looked preppy, but a lot more casual and approachable than he had in a suit.

Erin found herself wishing he was still ridiculously overdressed…so she wouldn't be noticing the big man's perfectly toned shoulders and chest.

"Your appointment isn't for another two hours," she said.

"I know." He flashed an apologetic grin that did funny things to her insides. "I've had some…*complications.* I was hoping we could get the measuring done a little earlier."

"I'm sorry." Erin indicated her happily married friend, glad to have an excuse to wait until her brother was on the premises, and could not only play chaperone, but distract them with his myriad questions and comments. "I have an appointment with Darcy next."

As determined as ever to get Erin back in the dating game, Darcy promptly volunteered, "I'll trade with you."

Mac grinned. "Oh…thanks! I really appreciate that."

"No problem." She beamed, sashaying toward the door. "See you both later."

After Darcy left, he turned back to Erin and pinned her with his gaze. Another shimmer of awareness sifted through her.

Erin thought about the property taxes coming due on the ranch and tried to focus on business. "Have you ever had custom footwear made before?" she asked, gesturing toward the stairs.

He fell into step behind her. "No."

Trying not to think of his eyes on her behind—how did she know what he was looking at as they climbed the stairs?—she took in an enervating breath and did her best to treat him like any other customer.

She turned at the top of the stairway and smiled. "The first thing is the measuring. If you'll have a seat—" she led him over to a straight-back chair "—and take off your shoes..."

Mac settled his large frame with grace while Erin pulled up a stool. Heart pounding, she attached a piece of paper to a clipboard and set it on the floor in front of him, then asked him to stand once again.

When he was on his feet, she slipped a hand around his ankle and guided his right foot onto the center of the paper. His socks were as fine a fabric as the rest of his clothes.

"How long have you been doing this?" Mac asked.

Glad to have something else to concentrate on other than him, she picked up a pencil and traced the outline of his foot on the paper. "I started learning the art of boot making when I was twelve. I was eighteen when I made my first pair, all on my own."

Erin slid another piece of paper onto the clipboard, marked it for the left foot and, holding that foot firmly in place, traced around it, too.

"And now your little brother is learning the art?"

Erin gestured for Mac to sit back down. She picked up his right foot and wrapped the measuring tape around the metatarsal bone just beneath his toes. "Nicholas can measure for the last—the replicated form of your foot that the boot is made to fit. And take orders, if the customer knows exactly what he or she wants, as most cowboys who come in here do." Erin paused to write down the numbers on the sheet of paper with the outline of Mac's right foot. "He's not interested in helping formulate a design or the actual crafting of the boot."

Mac watched as she measured the middle of his arch. "So it's just the two of you?"

Erin nodded. She grasped his foot and stretched it out, so his toes were pointed downward, then measured just above the center of his heel and around the ankle bone. "And the help we employ, like Darcy, who works here part-time. She says it's to support her custom-boot habit." Which, Erin knew, was pretty much true. Darcy had almost as many pairs of boots as Erin did.

Mac smiled, nodding at her to continue.

"Although my siblings and I all grew up helping out in the store."

Erin had him stand again. All business now, she asked, "Are you going to wear your pants inside your boots or over?" Because that would make a difference.

When he said, "Over," she guided his weight squarely over his foot, then measured around his calf. Finished, she recorded that figure, then guided him to sit down again so she could take the measurements of his left foot.

While she worked, Mac relaxed his foot in her grip, and asked casually, "Your family owns a ranch, too, don't they?"

Still aware of him in a way she definitely shouldn't be, Erin nodded, telling herself there would never be anything between her and this out-of-towner, no matter how many sparks his nearness generated. "The Triple Canyon Ranch," she answered.

Mac waited for her to finish writing down some stats

before saying, "It's my understanding the property hasn't been used for agricultural purposes in years."

Erin gestured for him to stand again. When he did, she knelt in front of him and wrapped the measuring tape around his left calf. "Not since my parents died, when I was twenty-three."

"I'd heard as much," he murmured.

Erin made a final notation and straightened, studying the expression on his face. Romantic fantasies faded as reality took over. She let her gaze slide over him and guessed wryly, "And you're thinking our ten thousand acres would be perfect for a wind farm."

Mac slid his feet into his shoes. "The topography is wide open, and rough enough to generate a lot of wind. It's tucked into a remote corner of Laramie County, yet within easy reach of the county power plant."

A trickle of unease went through her. "You've seen our property?" she asked in shock.

Guileless blue eyes held hers. "Via helicopter, yes."

"And that's why you wanted boots," she accused. "So you could talk me into selling the property to North Wind Energy?"

His gaze held hers without apology. "Or leasing, long-term, if your family would prefer."

Furious at having been played, Erin stood. "First of all, I don't own the property myself," she told him icily, carrying the clipboard over to the counter, wondering if she should shred all her notes right now. "I share the rights with my siblings."

Mac didn't seem the least bit put off. "I understand there are five of you."

He certainly had done his homework.

Erin lounged against the counter, her arms folded in front of her. "That's right. Sixteen-year-old Nicholas, whom you met the other day. Bridget and Bess, my twenty-two-year-old twin sisters, who are both finishing up nursing school at San Angelo State University. And my brother Gavin. He's thirty-three, a year younger than me, and is currently completing his residency in cardio-thoracic medicine." None of them were interested in agriculture, or the store. Nicholas just worked there part-time to earn spending money. But all of them shared an emotional attachment to the ranch house and the land four generations of Monroes had grown up on.

Mac continued, "I'd like to talk to all of you."

Erin just bet he would.

But before she could formulate a reply, the bell jingled on the first floor and then the front door slammed. "Mom!" Sammy and Stevie yelled in unison.

Saved by her sons. Relieved, Erin flashed a pointed smile at Mac. "I've got to go." She brushed past him and headed for the stairs.

He was right behind her. "We haven't finished."

"Oh, I think we have," she said over her shoulder, as cheerfully determined as he was.

The bell jangled again.

The door opened just as Erin reached the main floor. A young girl with messy blond curls—and an ice-cream cone in her hand—charged in, sobbing, "Daddy!" A uniformed chauffeur trailed behind her.

At the sight of the hopelessly distraught child wailing for her father, Erin's heart clenched in a way it hadn't in a good long while. Suddenly, it was all she could do not to burst into tears herself.

"Daddy!" the little girl yelled again, tears of indignation streaming down her face as the cone she was holding lost its top, and strawberry ice cream landed on the floor with a splat. "I'm tired of Texas!" The girl tossed the cone aside and stomped her foot. "I want to go home! Right now!"

TALK ABOUT BAD TIMING, Mac thought, while striding to the rescue.

"As you can see, despite your reassurances, this is not working," the uniformed young woman told him with an indignant sniff. "I am a chauffeur, not a babysitter."

No kidding. He should have followed his instincts and brought Heather into the store with him, despite the driver's assurances it would be okay. He'd figured the appointment would take just twenty or thirty minutes, long enough for him to set up a meeting with the whole Monroe clan.

But that hadn't happened, and now his little girl was in meltdown mode. Mac knelt and gathered his sobbing daughter into his arms. "Heather, honey, it's all right…." he soothed, holding her close.

"Daddy, you said this would be fun!" she cried.

Aware they had the attention of everyone in the store, he patted her back. "I thought watching a movie and eating ice cream in the limo would be fun for you," he said lamely.

Out of the corner of his eye, he couldn't help but notice Erin observing from the sidelines with a strangely paralyzed look on her face.

"But I want you to stay with me!" Heather clung to him all the tighter, shifting his focus back to his weeping daughter.

He could hardly blame her for being upset. She'd had way too much change in her life in the past few days. What she needed was normalcy, stability. Not that he seemed able to give her that at the moment.

The two boys who'd entered the store edged closer to Erin, their eyes fixed on Heather. The younger one elbowed his mom. "What's her problem?"

Heather turned to look at him. Her tears momentarily forgotten, she pushed away from Mac and demanded with equal curiosity, "Who's he?"

From the sidelines, a group of cowboys looking over a display of Wranglers shifted uncomfortably.

Cringing, Mac couldn't blame them. He hated emotional scenes, too.

Erin motioned for the salesclerk behind the counter to help the men. Her eyes glistening brightly, she stepped toward Mac and his little girl. "Hello, Heather," she said with a smile. "My name is Erin and this is my son Sammy. He's eight. This is my other son, Stevie. He's ten. How old are you?"

Heather sniffed, her misery fading fast. "I'm six."

"We have a toy corner in the back of the store. Would you like to see it?"

Heather looked at Mac. "Can I, Daddy?"

He released her. "Sure."

"Come on. We'll show you," Sammy said, reaching out and taking her hand.

Stevie fell into step beside them. "Mom, is it okay if we get our after-school snack?"

Erin blinked. For a moment there she'd been a million miles away, lost in her own thoughts as her sons quickly bonded with the little girl.

"Sure," Mac said again, when she looked at him for permission.

"You can have a snack," Erin told her boys, "but share whatever you get with Heather, too."

"Okay, Mom."

The children strode off, still hand in hand.

Although Mac couldn't help but wonder about the emotional expression that had flitted over Erin's face, he turned his attention to the mess his daughter had made. "Do you have anything I can clean this up with?" he asked.

Erin glanced at the strawberry ice cream puddled on the floor. "Don't worry about it." She pivoted and went to the counter, returning with a roll of paper towels and a bottle of cleaner. Mac couldn't help noticing how her hips swayed beneath her nicely fitted jeans, or the way her calico print shirt clung to her breasts as she knelt down.

Desire sifted through him, so fierce and unexpected it took him a minute to access some working brain cells. His body tightening with a demand that hadn't been met in way too long, he hunkered down beside her and caught her hand. "Let me do that."

Silky skin heated beneath his fingertips as she sucked in a startled breath. Their glances met as she studied him with big green eyes.

Damn, but she was pretty, Mac noted, despite his attempt to keep his interactions with her businesslike. She was feminine everywhere she should be. Delicate features, a heart-shaped face and upswept honey-blond curls only added to her womanly allure.

She was obviously successful—which he liked. Stubborn—which was probably going to make her harder to persuade. But persuade he would, Mac vowed. "I'll clean this up."

Her teeth raked across her soft, plump lower lip. "You really don't have to do that."

He gave her his most persuasive smile. "I insist."

The truth was, he wanted to do something else entirely with her.

But that wouldn't help him fulfill his agenda. And he'd do well to remember the *real* reason he was here....

Flustered, Erin handed him the necessary supplies and gave him room to work.

Not long after he had finished, the door jangled again. A group of ladies strolled in, followed by Erin's brother.

"Sorry I'm late, sis. I—" Nicholas stopped dead at the sight of Mac. "I thought you weren't coming till later."

Erin filled him in, "He switched appointments with Darcy, so I took his measurements for the last."

"What about the rest of the ordering process?" the teen asked.

"I'm going to do that later," Mac promised.

Nicholas's face fell in disappointment. "Then you won't be staying?"

Mac looked at his chauffeur, who was standing near the door, then back at Heather. Although his daughter was happily playing with Sammy and Stevie in the corner of the room, she could easily have another meltdown soon. "I have my daughter with me."

"I don't suppose you have dinner plans tonight?" Nicholas asked eagerly, before Erin could intervene. "Because if you don't, I sure would appreciate it if you and your daughter could come out to our ranch and eat with all of us."

Mac looked at Erin. Her cheeks were flushed and she didn't quite meet his eyes. "I wouldn't want to impose..." he said.

Oblivious to his sister's discomfort, Nicholas rushed on with teenage impetuousness. "It wouldn't be an imposition! We're always inviting people new to the community over for dinner. As Erin says, when you're already feeding seven or eight, what's one or two more?"

But this was different, Mac knew. She wouldn't want

him there with her entire family. On the other hand, it would be a perfect opportunity for him to speak with everyone at once. Find out how much work it would take to convince them his proposal was a good one.

The hint of discord in her eyes indicated she was realizing the exact same thing. "Nicholas!" Erin interjected quickly, "Let's not put Mr. Wheeler on the spot."

Or your sister, Mac thought. Although it was too late for that. He looked at his daughter, aware it was the first time he'd seen her smile in two days, and announced, "Actually, we'd love to come."

It would give him a chance to show Erin he wasn't a bad guy.

Nicholas grinned. "Is it okay if I invite a couple of my buddies from the environmental club, too?"

Mac looked back at his would-be hostess.

Seemingly as aware as he that everyone in the store had stopped to hear her answer, Erin flashed a smile, radiating a Texas-style hospitality that belied the cautiousness he could see in her gaze. "The more the merrier."

Or was it safety in numbers? Mac thought, wondering what would happen if the two of them were ever alone. Would the sparks continue to fly? Or would she ward him off with every ounce of grit she possessed?

"What time would you like us to be there?" he asked casually, and was rewarded with a faint blush of pink in her cheeks.

"Any time after seven would be good," she allowed.

"Great...see you then."

Heather didn't want to leave the store, but finally assented when she realized she would be seeing Stevie and Sammy again in a few hours, this time at their ranch.

"Daddy, will the ranch have animals?" she asked, after

he'd settled the bill with the limo driver and rented an SUV to get around instead.

Mac carried their suitcases into their room at the Laramie Inn. "I'm not sure."

"Can I have a dog?"

"Honey, we talked about this. As long as I'm traveling so much…"

Heather sighed, repeating his oft-said phrase, "It's just not practical."

"But when things settle down at work, and I'm not required to be on the road nearly as much, then I promise I *will* get you a puppy. Okay?"

Her expression turned glum.

Mac could tell she really didn't believe anything would ever change. She was still moody and quiet when they arrived at the Triple Canyon Ranch and drove through the black, wrought-iron gate.

In the distance, Mac could see the rocky ridges and deep canyons the property had been named after. Near the highway, the topography was flatter. Live oak trees lined either side of the paved lane that led to the big, sprawling ranch house. A pitched brown roof draped majestically over the eaves. The second story was covered with dark brown cedar shakes, while the lower level was painted a light cocoa color. Bright white trim set off the windows and the dark brown front door. A covered porch spanned the width of the house, with a bench swing and matching chairs providing a comfortable seating area.

It was a house built for multiple generations, with a pasture full of horses, a barn and stable nearby.

Sammy and Stevie were shooting basketballs through a hoop next to the driveway. They waited until Mac parked the SUV, then dashed toward them. "Do you know how to play basketball?" they asked Heather.

She shook her head.

"Want to learn?"

She shrugged shyly. "Maybe."

Erin walked out onto the porch.

Mac was surprised to see she'd let her hair down. It glowed like rich honey in the early evening light, and flowed over her shoulders in thick, gorgeous curls. She was still in jeans, but had taken off the calico shirt and put on a short-sleeved, scoop-necked T-shirt that matched the peachy hue of her cheeks. Somehow, she seemed less businesswoman, more easygoing Mom. But every bit as sexy as before.

"Guys, go easy on her, okay? You've got twenty minutes until you have to wash up."

"Okay, Mom!" Stevie answered.

Her smile cordial, Erin ushered Mac inside. The interior was both rustic and homey, with wide-plank wood floors, colorful Southwestern rugs and sun-washed yellow walls. Big, comfortable-looking furniture was accented with lots of Texana memorabilia and family photos.

She came closer in a drift of lilac perfume. "What can I get you to drink?" she asked almost too pleasantly.

Mac reminded himself he wasn't here to challenge her hospitality or to put the moves on her. He leaned against the white limestone fireplace that went all the way up to the cathedral ceiling of the main living area. "Iced tea, if you have it."

She pivoted and headed to the kitchen. "Coming right up."

Mac followed, his eyes on her hips.

Erin paused to check on a casserole baking in the oven. "Nicholas went to pick up a couple of his friends. They'll be back shortly, so prepare yourself for the nonstop questions about your line of work."

Mac had figured as much. He watched her plunk ice into a glass, noticing the lack of wedding ring on her hand. "What about the rest of your siblings?" *And her husband? Where was he? Was she divorced? Widowed?* Belatedly, he realized he should have done better research on the alluring woman in front of him.

"Bridget and Bess won't be here. They're staying on campus in San Angelo, studying for an exam. Gavin should be home from the hospital soon, though." Erin met Mac's gaze for a long, highly charged moment.

"I look forward to meeting him."

She nodded and handed him his iced tea, careful not to let their fingers touch, then turned away. "I'm going to check on the kids."

Mac trailed her back to the front of the house, where she glanced out a window. And promptly turned as pale as a ghost.

Chapter Three

For a moment, it was as if Erin had hurtled back through time, to what might have been. Heart constricting, she forced her eyes away from the sight of Heather riding bikes with the boys.

She had to stop doing this, she told herself sternly. Stop thinking, remembering, wishing things had been different....

Because they weren't different—and never would be, no matter how she yearned to go back, find a different outcome.

Her throat aching with the effort it took to hold back a sob, she swung away from the window.

Mac was staring at her, his handsome face creased with concern. "What's wrong?"

Wishing he could pull her into his arms and comfort her—the way he'd comforted his daughter when she'd been upset—Erin rushed back through the house. Mac was right behind her.

The logical side of her knew he deserved an explanation. This was the second time she'd reacted emotionally, in just a few hours. Because she couldn't let go of the past.

She lifted a palm. "It's nothing."

"The hell it is," he countered gruffly, refusing to let her cut and run.

Feeling her body heat under his probing gaze, she tried again. "I just…I didn't expect—" Her voice broke, and she swallowed. He wasn't going to give up until he knew, so she shook her head, forced herself to go on. "Angelica…"

"Who's Angelica?" he asked gently.

Hot, bitter tears pushed at the back of her eyes. Her throat ached so badly she could barely speak. "My daughter. She died two years ago, when she was six." Erin grabbed hold of the kitchen counter and shut her eyes. She could feel Mac next to her, hovering, patiently waiting for her to confide in him.

He moved closer, and Erin felt a wave of comforting strength emanating from him. Eventually she choked out, "That was Angelica's bike that Heather is riding."

"Would you like me to ask her to stop?" Mac's voice sounded a little raspy, too.

Swallowing hard, Erin opened her eyes and turned toward him. "No, of course not. Not when they're all having such a good time. In fact, I haven't seen my boys look so happy in a long time. Not since they had a little sister to play with."

Mac took a look at the photos strewn across the top of the kitchen hutch. One of a much younger Erin, and her brothers and sisters, standing with their parents. Another of Erin and her husband, surrounded by their three kids. The photos of Erin's daughter caught his attention, too. Mac paused in shock. "Our daughters look so much alike," he murmured.

Erin nodded, her heart constricting again. Heather and Angelica might have been sisters. The two little girls had the same thick, curly blond hair and piquant faces, the same exuberance and zest for life. The only difference being that Erin's child was dead now, while Mac's was still very much alive.

Erin couldn't help but envy him that.

He took her hand and led her into the family room. Too overwrought to protest, she followed numbly. "What happened?" He guided her to the sofa and sank down beside her.

Erin made no protest when he slung a comforting arm around her shoulders. She didn't often talk about this, but knew she needed to tonight. With him. She turned and looked into Mac's eyes, still stunned about the unexpectedness of it all. "She had cancer."

He tightened his grip on her. His eyes were steady. Calm. And so filled with tenderness and compassion, she wanted to weep. "How long was she sick?" he asked quietly.

Erin swallowed again. "Ten months." Ten hellishly long, yet way-too-short months.

"How did you find out?"

Determined not to lose it again, she slid a shaking hand over her thigh. "The bike Heather's riding..." Mac's brow furrowed and Erin forced herself to continue, "Angelica learned to ride when she was four. It only took her a couple of weeks to master it without the training wheels, and she was so proud of herself. So happy to be out riding around the driveway with her big brothers. Then one day, when she was five and a half—" Erin's voice broke at the memory of that last "completely normal" day "—she fell off for no reason anyone could see, and scraped up her hands and knees."

Mac grimaced in sympathy as the memories engulfed Erin.

"That night she started complaining about her head hurting. Even though she'd been wearing a helmet, I was scared. I thought she might have hurt something in the fall, so I took her to the E.R. and had her checked out just to be sure."

The sorrow Erin felt, then and now, was mirrored in Mac's eyes. "And that's when they found the tumor that was affecting the 'balance' area of her brain," she concluded brokenly.

Mac drew her closer, until she was pressed against his side. His irises darkened. "You must have been terrified."

Erin had been. Knowing she needed to continue unburdening herself, as much as he needed to listen, she leaned into his comforting warmth. "My husband and I took Angelica to MD Anderson in Houston. They did surgery and chemotherapy and radiation. She lost all her beautiful hair." *And had cried and cried and cried, until she decided she liked being bald, anyway.* "For a while, we thought she was going to be okay." Erin released a shuddering sigh, beginning to feel her heart go numb again at the memory. "But then the tumor came back… and Angelica died about three months after that."

"I'm so sorry." Mac embraced her. For a moment, Erin let herself be held against the solid warmth of his chest.

Aware she could get a little too used to that, she drew away. Exhaled again.

Mac let her go. He looked at her left hand, taking in the absence of a ring. "What happened to your husband?"

Needing some space, after confiding so much, Erin stood and began to roam the room. In a choked voice, she admitted, "The same thing that happens to a lot of parents who have terminally-ill kids." She pushed away the hurt and disappointment that lingered. "G.W. discovered he couldn't handle the loss. And he left."

Mac had the same incredulous, disapproving reaction as most of their family and friends. "You're divorced."

It was more a statement than a question.

She nodded. "For over a year."

He looked as if he wanted to punch something. "Where is he now?"

"All over the place. He's a geologist. He works as a scout for an oil company."

"Does he have contact with your sons?" Mac asked.

"Once every month or so he'll call or come by, usually without warning." She shrugged. "He sends child-support checks, though. I suppose we ought to be grateful for that."

Mac pondered that. "How do your kids feel?"

Bitterness welled in her heart. It was one thing to be abandoned herself, another to watch her kids suffer through it. "How do you think? First they lose their sister. Then their dad leaves, too."

As Mac watched her in silence, guilt washed over her. It wasn't as if any of this were his fault. "I'm sorry. I didn't mean to be so short with you."

"Hey." His lips quirked ruefully. "I'm the one who should be apologizing, for asking such an intrusive question. It's just...Sammy and Stevie are such great kids, and it's hard to imagine anyone walking away from them."

Erin felt the same.

Silence fell once again.

She peered at Mac through narrowed lashes, studying him curiously. "What about you? You're here with your daughter, no wife in tow."

"Cassandra died of a pulmonary embolism two and a half years ago," he said gruffly.

"I'm sorry."

He nodded, accepting her condolences.

Erin resisted the urge to comfort him with a touch, a hug, relying instead on a heartfelt look. "Is Heather still having a rough time?"

"She was so young, she doesn't remember a lot about

her mother. But she misses her best friend, whose family used to take care of her when I was on the road."

Erin focused on the past tense. "Used to?"

He exhaled roughly and shoved a hand through his hair. "Joel was promoted. He and Anna and their daughter, Stella, moved to Kansas last week. I hired a live-in nanny, but Heather pitched a fit. So I went back to Philadelphia, released the nanny from our contract and brought my daughter back here to Texas with me."

"You couldn't just stay home in Philadelphia for a while?"

He shook his head. "There's too much riding on this wind-farm deal."

Erin let out a breath. "I see." Obviously, Mac was one of those guys who would always put work first. Ahead of family, relationships, everything. Which was too bad for his daughter. Like Erin's sons, Heather needed her one remaining parent, now more than ever.

Mac squinted at Erin, his mood suddenly as pensive as hers. "I'm not sure you do understand…"

Just then the front door slammed. Nicholas and four of his buddies sauntered in.

The anticipated questions started for Mac. And that, Erin found, was the end of that.

By the time Erin had dinner ready, Gavin had dragged himself in the door, after a thirty-six-hour shift at the hospital. His eyes rimmed with fatigue, he said, "Storm's coming, sis," and went straight to bed.

Thinking they'd better eat soon if all her guests were to get home safely, Erin went out to the porch and rang the dinner bell.

Stevie and Sammy put all three bikes in the garage and then dashed in, followed by Heather.

"Sit between us. That way you can be next to both of us," Stevie urged after they'd washed their hands.

Another arrow to Erin's heart. And yet…it was obvious that her boys hadn't looked this happy and content in ages. She hadn't realized until this very moment how much they needed another little girl to fill the void left in their lives, in the wake of Angelica's passing.

In the distance, Erin heard thunder. Spurred into action, she carried the piping hot baking dish of King Ranch casserole to the table, then returned to the stove for the big bowls of Mexican rice and refried beans. In honor of their youngest guest, Erin had also prepared a very kid-friendly version of mac'n'cheese, green beans and applesauce.

As expected, Heather opted for the familiar, when it came time for her to choose.

"So how long are you going to be in Laramie?" Nicholas asked Mac as everyone spooned food onto their plates.

Mac spread his napkin on his lap. "Until I get approval from the county for a wind farm—and a ranch to put it on."

"You do know," Nicholas volunteered, "that we're not running cattle here anymore."

Erin gave him a cautioning glance.

"So I heard," Mac said, taking the opening.

Nicholas looked at Erin, the dollar signs flashing in his eyes. "We might want to consider it."

And, Erin reflected silently, *we might not.* The last thing she needed was any connection at all to a man who was already on his way out of her life. Or would be, once his job here in Laramie County was done.

Nicholas's friend Bobby's cell phone rang. He glanced at the caller ID. "Uh-oh, that's my mom." Rising from the table, he walked off, phone to his ear. "Okay, okay. I'll talk to Nicholas and get moving right now."

Bobby came back, a sheepish look on his face. "My mom says I've got to get home before the storm hits. I hate to eat and run, but..."

The other boys shoveled in the last of their dinners and rose.

Erin looked at Nicholas. "Drive safe. And come right home after you drop everyone off."

"Will do, sis." He ushered his friends out.

The rest of them finished eating. As Erin rose to clear the table and get dessert, thunder rumbled again in the distance.

She took the peach cobbler out of the oven, then flipped on the TV to check the local weather report.

Mac set a stack of dishes next to the sink, then moved to stand beside her. "Everything okay?"

Maybe not, Erin thought. She nodded at the Doppler radar on the screen. As much as she hated to be a nervous Nellie... "Actually, Mac, there is reason to be concerned." She pointed out the big wave of green and the smaller cells of yellow and red. "Storms out here can be—" she thought about Heather, who was listening intently, and chose her next words carefully "—rather, um, virulent."

Mac's lifted his eyebrows. "Should we be on our way, too?"

Heather's face fell. She looked at Stevie and Sammy, who seemed equally disappointed. Erin took another look at the TV screen. As much as she hated to admit it... "It's probably too late for that, given the direction you're headed." Nicholas's friends all lived on ranches close by. Mac had a nearly forty-minute drive to the Laramie Inn, in good weather. This wasn't that.

Since she had a sneaking suspicion that he didn't

believe her, Erin led him out to the back porch. Sure enough, about a mile or so away they could see dark clouds stretching from sky to ground. Lightning flashed and thunder rumbled. In the yard, the wind was whipping up, rattling the window screens and bending the trees.

Mac's dismissive glance let her know he wasn't worried. "The SUV I rented has all-wheel drive."

"The problem is the low water crossings," Erin returned, knowing spring storms in Texas could be fiercer than he knew. "A lot of the creek beds are dry and filled with debris. They'll wash over quickly and the roads will likely be flooded till morning."

A fact that made leaving the ranch extremely dangerous. "You and Heather would really be safer staying here."

MAC HAD EXPECTED a lot of things this evening. An argument over the advisability of a wind farm as a solution to Laramie County's current energy shortage. A division between Monroe family members, some wanting to sell out, others not. Even some minor dickering over the price his company was willing to pay.

However, he hadn't expected to hear about the most difficult times of Erin's life. Or to have dinner in such a warm and homey atmosphere. Or to see his own little girl, who was so often lonely, fit right in with Erin's boys.

It all made him want to keep coming back to the Triple Canyon Ranch.

And not on business.

Which was why he should head back to town. Now.

"That's very kind of you to offer," he told Erin. "But you really don't have to put us up for the night."

She gave him a wry once-over, letting him know what a gringo she deemed him to be. Mac found himself grinning back. Chemistry sizzled between them, more electric than the supercharged air outside. Wanting her, Mac knew, would be a lot more dangerous to him than a simple thunderstorm.

"Texas hospitality kind of says I do," Erin quipped. "After all, it wouldn't be neighborly of me to turn you and your daughter out in this."

Mac looked away from the softness of her lips. He needed to be a gentleman here. "I appreciate your concern, Erin, but I assure you, I've driven in storms before. And before you point out that the country roads can be confusing around here, I'd like to remind you that I found my way to the ranch. I can find my way back to town." Mostly, Mac thought, because his smartphone had GPS. Had he relied only on road signs—which were few and far between—and the directions she had given him, he'd have been up a creek.

The power flickered briefly as Erin led the way back into the house. The kids had moved from the kitchen table to a jigsaw puzzle set up on the game table in the family room.

"The point is, you don't have to. We have plenty of room here. And..." Erin cast another look at his daughter, who was sitting with her head propped up on her hand "Heather looks exhausted."

Mac couldn't argue that point. She did appear tired. Barely able to keep her eyes open.

Lightning zigzagged across the sky, followed by a house-rattling clap of thunder. "How about I show you the guest quarters before you make up your mind?"

Reminding himself that he was doing this for his daughter, Mac nodded and followed Erin up the stairs.

Once again it had been a mistake to let her go first. All he could see when he glanced up was the graceful sway of her hips as she climbed the steps. The sexy spill of her hair, brushing across her shoulders. The hem of her T-shirt caressing her slender waist. Lower still were long, sleek thighs encased in the sky-blue jeans, and sexy calves disappearing into the tops of her custom peacock-blue boots.

Damn, but she was one attractive woman.

Oblivious to his admiring glance, Erin turned at the newel post and led the way down a long hallway. They passed what must be her sons' rooms, and then paused in the doorway of a third.

It was sparsely decorated and painted a pale pink.

Mac had a feeling he knew whose room this had been, so he kept a respectful distance as Erin pulled out a trundle bed that was half the height of the other mattress. "You'll be able to sleep right next to Heather," she said, patting the crisp sheets. "Whether on the lower or higher bed is up to you. And the boys' rooms are right next door, so I imagine that will comfort Heather."

Erin was right—it would. Mac studied her expression as the power flickered briefly once again.

Thunder rumbled closer.

"You're sure it's okay?" he rasped, wishing she would give him some reason not to want her.

"I wouldn't have offered if it wasn't," she murmured, her eyes telling him she was as affected by his presence as he was by hers.

They exchanged glances, and an intimacy Mac hadn't expected welled up between them. Decision made, he ignored the punch of desire in his gut. Just because he felt it didn't mean he had to act on it.

He nodded agreeably. "Then we'll bunk here for the night."

Chapter Four

Erin was curled up in a corner of the living room sofa, sketch pad on her lap, when Mac finally came back downstairs nearly an hour later. His hair was rumpled, his shirttail out, shoes off, and the sleeves of his shirt were rolled up to the elbow. The sleepy look in his eyes indicated he might have briefly nodded off, too, after tucking Heather into bed. Erin smiled, appreciating the fact that he'd cared enough to stay with his daughter until she fell asleep.

"Nicholas get home okay?" he asked in a low, husky voice that warmed her inside and out.

Telling herself they were just being nice to each other because they were stuck here together for the duration of the storm, Erin nodded. "He's upstairs doing homework." She gazed up at Mac. "Can I get you anything?"

A sexy glimmer shone briefly in his eyes, as if he had an answer to that. One she wouldn't want to hear. "I'm good. Thanks." His glance trailed over the red-white-and-blue lady's boot, emblazoned with stars and stripes, that she'd been designing. "What's this?"

"A limited edition woman's boot that will be prototyped in time for Independence Day."

"Nice." Mac sat down beside her on the sofa and

propped his feet up on the coffee table. "How many copies will you make?"

Damn, but he smelled good. Like soap and man and an ever-so-faint hint of expensive cologne.

Erin tried not to think about what it would be like to kiss him, which would have been a whole lot easier if he wasn't giving off so many pheromones and didn't have such erotically sculpted lips. Not that she was noticing… "We'll stop at two hundred."

"How long will it take to sell out?"

How long would it take for her to squelch the desire she hadn't felt since she couldn't remember when? "Once I put a pair up on the website and in the store? About a week."

He continued to study the design. "I like it," he murmured. "It's…"

"Patriotic?"

"Very," he drawled as he settled more comfortably beside her, his elbow briefly brushing hers. "And speaking of boots, when do you want to finish the order for mine?"

Erin put her sketchbook aside. "No time like the present."

"Great!" He beamed.

Determined to resist the disarming smile he sent her way, she rose and strode purposefully toward the armoire. Maybe it was best they keep their mind on business, rather than anything personal. Heaven knew they had shared enough earlier in the evening.

"Ready to get started?" she asked, returning with an array of samples and a book of color photos.

He nodded. "You really love this, don't you?"

Erin replied with a shrug, "I love the design work, helping customers figure out what they want and turning their wishes into reality."

"Do you actually make the boot, too?" His voice was low and gravelly and sexy as hell.

Erin sat down beside him. "Sometimes I do." She'd probably make Mac's, because of the time constraints. "But for the most part, the four artists Monroe's employs make the lasts and do the actual cutting and sewing and buffing in their home studios." Erin opened up her satchel. "Any idea what color boot you want?"

"Dark brown."

No surprise there. She fanned out a bunch of samples.

Mac stared at them, as flummoxed as most men when confronted with all those choices. "I had no idea there were so many different shades of dark brown."

She pointed out the undertones in several of the shades. "There's also a difference in texture. Crocodile or lizard skin is bumpy." She placed his hand over the hide, so he could feel it, then moved it to the next. "Kangaroo is a little softer. Cowhide is more durable."

"Which would you suggest?"

Erin shrugged. "Depends on whether you plan to use them for outdoor activity or the boardroom."

"Both."

"In that case..." She suggested a leather that was both soft and durable.

Mac smiled. "I like it."

"Now for the shape. Do you want a full round roper toe? A semiround one? Or something more pointed, like a cut-back toe?" She showed him pictures. "Or perhaps something more rectangular in shape, like a French toe with a wide boxed end?"

"I prefer the wide boxed end. No scalloping or fancy stitching, though."

Erin reached for her sketch pad. "How about something like this?" Sensing from what she already knew of him that he wouldn't want anything too fussy, she drew a medallion and wrinkle across the toe of the boot, and a simple filigree around the top. The overall effect was understated and elegant.

"That looks good," Mac said, satisfied.

"Do you want your initials on them? We can put them on the ear pulls, where they generally won't be seen, or on the front inside quarter panel or the heel."

"I think the pulls would be good."

Erin made a note of that, then got out her calculator. She wrote up a bill of sale, then handed him the final tally. "We usually ask for half up front."

"I'll drop off a check at the shop tomorrow." Which meant she'd be seeing him yet again.

Erin glanced at the clock, noting it was after eleven. Rain was still pouring down outside. For a long beat, no one said anything. He seemed as reluctant to call it a night as she was. "I had no idea it was so late," she said.

Mac stretched lazily. "Me, either." His voice was low, gravelly and sexy as hell.

She moved her gaze away from his sinewy shoulders and chest. There was no use dreaming about what was never going to happen. What she would never let happen. She swallowed around the sudden dryness in her throat. Emotional barriers firmly in place, she asked politely, "Can I get you anything before I go up to bed?"

He smiled. "I'm good."

"Well." Her pulse quickening in reaction to his nearness, she closed her heavy satchel. "You know where the kitchen is. *Mi casa es su casa* and all that. Help yourself to anything you want or need. And I'll see you in the morning."

He nodded, his easy acknowledgment cocooning her in

warmth. "Good night. And Erin?" He held her eyes until her heart skipped a beat. "Thanks for the hospitality."

This wasn't the end of a date, even if it suddenly felt like one. Ignoring the telltale rush of heat inside her, Erin cleared her throat. "No problem."

He smiled again, even more gratefully.

Tingling, she forced herself to turn away and head for the stairs. She was halfway to the second-floor landing when everything suddenly went dark.

MAC HAD THOUGHT the evening could hold no more surprises. Just showed how little he knew.

"Mac?" Erin's soft voice came out of the pitch-black interior of the sprawling ranch house.

He pushed away the notion that she could easily become something to him. "Yeah?"

"Need a flashlight?" she asked.

"It would help."

Damn, but it was black out here, with the rain still teeming down outside. No light whatsoever, anywhere, not even a distant flash of lightning. Mac put his hands out in front of him, wishing for night-vision goggles, and trying to feel his way.

"Where are you?" Erin's voice sounded closer.

Good question. "Somewhere between the foyer and the middle of the living room," he replied, hoping that Heather—and the other kids—would sleep through this. He didn't want his daughter in another meltdown.

"Stay where you are," Erin advised calmly. "I'll come and get you."

"So, is this one of those rolling brownouts I've been hearing about?"

"Given the fact we've had no lightning in the immediate area, I'd have to guess yes."

The only upside of this situation was the sensuality of hearing her voice in the darkness, so soft and sweet and helpful. Mac had always loved a woman who was good in an emergency. He exhaled. "If that's what this is, how long is it going to last?"

"Thirty minutes." As Erin's voice came closer, he inhaled a drift of lilac perfume. "Maybe more. Maybe less." Without warning, her palm hit him in the center of his chest.

He savored her body heat. "And now you've found me."

"Sorry." She dropped her hand, stepped back.

He still couldn't see her, but he could hear the uneven meter of her breathing. His body tensing with need, he inhaled the flowery fragrance of her skin and hair. He had to rein in his fantasies here. "Now what?"

"The flashlights are in the kitchen."

Mac figured it would be better not to crash into anything else, especially something—or someone—soft and feminine and incredibly enticing. "Lead the way."

She touched his chest again, tentatively this time. "Take my hand."

He was glad she didn't grope for his palm, given the difference in their heights. No telling what she might have found.

He wrapped his hand around hers and fell into step behind her, or tried to. They hadn't gone more than five paces when she bumped into something and stumbled back into him, knocking him off balance, too. They would have fallen if he hadn't clamped an arm across her body and caught her against him, swift and hard. Unfortunately, the difference in their heights meant his forearm landed on the soft swell of her breasts.

His reaction was immediate. "Sorry," he murmured

quickly, loosening his grip as soon as he was sure she was steady on her feet.

Sensing her embarrassment in the silence that followed, he said, "I didn't mean to, uh…"

"Touch me that way?" she finished, with a trace of humor.

Mac winced in the darkness. "Right."

Unfortunately, now he knew how warm and womanly her breasts felt. The memory would stay with him, probably all night. He shifted, trying to ease the pressure at the front of his jeans.

"Put your hand out and take mine," she commanded.

When their fingers reconnected, he could feel the heat in her skin. "Let's keep going," she directed. "We're almost there."

Mac sucked in a breath. "I'm right behind you."

They moved forward, Erin holding on to him with one hand, feeling her way forward with the other. Eventually, they made it down the hallway to the kitchen. She let go of him, and opened a drawer.

Mac listened as she rummaged through the contents, muttering in dismay.

"What is it?" he asked.

Erin groaned. "The flashlights aren't here! The boys must have taken them to play with."

"So now what?"

Exasperated, she laid out their options. "Stay here in the kitchen and try and feel our way to the chairs at the table? Go back to the living room and wait it out there? Or try to make it up the stairs to bed. Without crashing into something and waking the entire household?"

"Those are our only options?"

She huffed. "Unless you can think of something else to do."

Actually, Mac could. Not, he reminded himself sternly, that making a pass at her was one of the options…

This was a business situation.

Or at least it had been…until they had started sharing personal stories and whiling away the time together.

Then it had become something else.

Something a lot more…treacherous.

Erin groaned and let out a nervous laugh. "Forget I said that."

The gentlemanly side of Mac knew he should. Only trouble was, he wasn't feeling particularly chivalrous right now. He was feeling…turned on. And she was, too, otherwise her mind wouldn't have gone in the exact same direction his had.

The direction that would land them in each other's arms.

"Actually," Mac said gruffly, turning toward her and gathering her closer, "I don't think I will."

Then, going on instinct, he slowly lowered his head.

ERIN HAD KNOWN this kiss was coming. Known it long enough to avoid being alone with him. But she hadn't.

Instead, she had invited it.

Why?

Because something about him attracted her and made her want to lose herself in him. In this.

And lose herself she did, as she opened her mouth to the inviting pressure of his.

He tasted so good. So dark and male. The strength of his chest pressed against hers. His thighs were rock hard, the rest of him just as impatient for more.

And that, above anything, told Erin she needed to stop this. Now.

Only she couldn't.

This was the most alive she had felt in a very long time.

And had it not been for a sudden beam of light flashing across their bodies, who knew how long it would have gone on?

THE LAST THING MAC EXPECTED when he took Erin in his arms was to be busted by the intrusive beam of a flashlight.

But that was what happened as Gavin walked into the kitchen and caught them pressed up against each other in a steamy lip-lock.

Reluctantly, Mac broke off the kiss and lifted his head from hers.

Dropping her hands from his chest, Erin stepped away.

Gavin looked at his sister, his brow lifted in silent inquiry.

She gazed back, angry and defiant. Not to mention embarrassed.

"Everything okay here?" Gavin asked finally, shifting the plastic casing so the flashlight became a lantern.

It was a minute ago, Mac wanted to say.

Figuring this was family business—and he should stay out of it—he remained silent.

"Do you know where the rest of the flashlights are?" Erin asked, her gaze averted from Gavin's probing look.

His body tense with a disapproval mostly directed at Mac, he nodded. "There are two in the cabinet above the washing machine. The rest are upstairs in the boys' rooms, next to their beds."

Erin disappeared into the laundry room, then returned with two flashlights in hand. She handed one to Mac.

"Are all the kids still asleep?" she asked Gavin.

"So far. I even looked in on Nicholas. He's snoozing away."

"Well…" Erin inhaled deeply, then turned and looked at Mac. "I'm going to call it a night."

He nodded. "See you tomorrow."

After she headed up the stairs, Gavin continued staring at him. "I gather you've got something to say?" Mac asked.

"You guessed right." A muscle worked in his cheek. "My sister's been through enough. The last thing she needs in her life is another guy who's not going to be around for the long haul."

Much as he hated to admit it, Mac knew Gavin had a point.

"It was just a kiss."

Gavin's jaw tightened. "Maybe to you. She hasn't given any guy the time of day since her ex left."

Mac hadn't dated in a very long time, either. And he sure as hell hadn't taken any woman in his arms and kissed her soundly.

He swallowed. "It's not my intention to hurt your sister."

Gavin shook his head. "Then I suggest you stick to business, and leave it at that."

Reluctantly, Mac gave ground. "You're right. No sense starting something that can't go anywhere. So maybe it's best we get down to business." Mac looked at Gavin, man to man, figuring the sooner he achieved his goals, the better. "Hopefully, you can help me with that."

ERIN STARED AT GAVIN just after eight the next morning. She'd been out taking care of the horses. By the time she got back to the house, Mac and his daughter had already left. They'd gotten directions back to town via an alternate route that avoided any flooded crossings. Erin's boys were upstairs brushing their teeth.

Nicholas had gone on to school.

Erin wasn't sure how she felt about missing Mac's departure. Seeing him probably would have been awkward after the sizzling kiss they had shared. Especially since she hadn't been able to stop thinking about it all night. Even when she'd finally closed her eyes and drifted off to sleep, she had woken up reliving the emotion of that moment.

She hadn't felt so aroused in what seemed like forever. Hadn't even been sure she could feel desire like that again.

Now she knew.

She still had plenty of untapped passion, ready and raring to go. And now Mac Wheeler knew it, too. As did her brother Gavin.

Erin went to the sink to wash her hands. "What did you and Mac talk about last night?" She had heard them conversing long after she had turned in. Their tone had been cordial, matter-of-fact, whereas she had still been in turmoil.

"I told him to stay away from you."

Erin squirmed. "Thanks."

"You're welcome."

"I was being sarcastic."

"Noted."

Erin folded her arms. "What did Mac say?"

"He agreed kissing you was a bad idea."

Her lips quirked. "Let me guess… And promised not to do it again?"

"We agreed, since he'll be leaving soon, and you have enough on your plate, that the two of you should stick to business. Which is why we have a family meeting tonight. Adults only, so you'll need to get a sitter for your boys, and it'd be nice if Mac's daughter could hang out with them, too."

Not sure she liked the idea of the two men joining forces, Erin asked, "Why is Mac going to be at our family meeting?"

Gavin filled his travel mug with coffee. "He wants to talk to us all about putting a wind farm on our ranch. He wanted to do it over dinner at one of the restaurants in town, but I said that wasn't necessary. So we're going to meet at Travis Anderson's law office instead."

Erin blinked. As the oldest, she considered herself the head of the family. And therefore used to calling the shots. "You asked our family attorney to sit in on this?"

"Travis is an expert in energy and property law."

Erin wasn't arguing that. She just didn't see the necessity of any of this, whether Mac Wheeler wanted it or not. "I'm not interested in selling the ranch."

"Well, the rest of us are, which means you owe us the courtesy of hearing Mac out."

ERIN CAUGHT UP WITH MAC early that afternoon, when she saw him coming out of the Wagon Wheel Restaurant with four of the county commissioners.

The two women and two men were deep in conversation with him, and appeared to be listening intently to what he had to say. All were smiling when they shook hands and parted ways. Mac was really making inroads, even in khakis, a button-down oxford-cloth shirt and loafers.

Not wanting to think what he could accomplish if he ever fully assimilated into a bona fide Texan, Erin continued down the sidewalk toward him. She inhaled a jerky breath, trying not to self-combust. Not easy, when all she could seem to do, now that they were within touching distance, was remember their kiss.

She couldn't help wondering if he was thinking the same thing.

She lifted her chin. "Got a minute?"

He favored her with a half smile. "Actually, you're just the lady I was hoping to see. I was headed to the store to give you a check for the down payment on the boots."

Erin glanced across the street. Some roughnecks from Prairie Natural Gas, the company that supplied gas to the power plant, were standing in front of several beat-up trucks, talking and looking their way. Not surprisingly, they seemed as interested in Mac as everyone else in the area was. Probably because their company would expand their business in Laramie County if he failed, and lose ground if he was successful. Aware that none of the men looked familiar, Erin turned back to Mac with a cool smile. "I'd rather talk privately."

He shrugged, his manner not nearly as businesslike. "You want to sit in my SUV?"

What speculation that would bring! Erin glanced around, assessing the options. "Let's walk over to the park across the street." She could pretend she was showing him something.

Mac glanced behind him, and his brow creased with concern. "Have those men been bothering you?"

His protectiveness rankled. "No. Why do you ask?"

He slid a hand beneath her elbow, ready to take care of her, anyway. "You seemed…a little on edge when you were looking at them."

She let him grasp her arm for a moment, so as not to look like an overreactive idiot to anyone watching, then casually pried herself loose, her skin still tingling from his touch. “I was wondering if they were following *you* around.”

“Maybe. Then again—” Mac mimicked her Southern drawl as his handsome face took on a Texas-size grin “—maybe we’re all just going to the same places. We’re definitely all bunking at the Laramie Inn, at least since I got back.”

Texas was a friendly place, Laramie County even more hospitable. Yet Erin knew things could get ugly fast when large sums of money were involved, no matter what state you were in. Luckily, Mac looked like he could take of himself, and then some.

She didn’t want to see anyone go after him. And there was his adorable little daughter to consider, too.

“Where is Heather this morning?” Erin had expected to see her with Mac.

“School. She was enrolled in a Montessori program in Philadelphia, so it was easy enough to get her transferred into the one here. Because it’s a self-paced curriculum, she should be able to finish out first grade here in Texas, before we head back to Philly.”

If Erin ever needed another reminder he was leaving again, this was it. Which was another reason she shouldn’t get involved. Last thing she needed was to fall for another man who would leave her in the dust.

“I’m still looking for a furnished house or apartment to rent,” Mac continued as they walked over to the park, “but that’s not so easy. Seems no one wants to rent for one to two months. If you hear of anything…”

Erin nodded. “I’ll put the word out, let you know if anything turns up.”

“There it is. That legendary Texas hospitality again.”

Erin returned his smile. It would be so easy to get lost in that charm. In him.

"So what did you want to discuss with me?" Mac asked.

Erin stopped short of the stone-and-glass monument that contained the framed map of the downtown Laramie historic district as well as directions to other popular tourist destinations in the area. She pretended to show him something. "Why did you kiss me last night?"

He studied the flush in her cheeks. "Do I need a reason, beside the obvious?"

"That's not an answer," she said stiffly.

Mac's blue eyes took on a mischievous gleam. "Okay, then. Why did *you* kiss *me?*"

Because, Erin thought, *I had been wanting to kiss you all evening, and it seemed like a good idea at the time. And because you make me feel incredibly reckless and alive whenever I'm near you. After years of feeling numb inside, I suddenly want to feel like a woman again. I want to feel desired. And that scares the heck out of me, even as it appears to energize you.*

"Did your hitting on me have anything to do with selling me on the wind farm idea?" *Because if that was the case...*

Mac's consternation quickly turned to pique. "I haven't slept my way up the ladder, if that's what you're intimating."

"What about to a specific deal?" Erin persisted. Mac was ambitious, charming and oh, so good-looking. He oozed testosterone. Not to mention being single and in a very competitive field. Erin knew there were sales execs who would use whatever they had at their disposal to close a deal, and then move on to the next. Her ultrasuccessful ex-husband had been one of them.

Mac scoffed. "Let me get this straight. You think I

need to bed a woman to persuade her that dealing with me and the company I represent would be good business?"

I think, given the way you kissed me, you could persuade a woman of damn near anything if you ever got her into bed.

Erin struggled not to flush. "I'm just saying there are better ways to get what you want around here than by bolstering someone's ego."

"And here I thought you were a straight-talker," he teased.

"I am very direct."

"Then maybe you can answer this for me." He looked her square in the eye. "If I were to pursue you romantically, would it make you more inclined to listen to me? Or less?"

"Neither."

"Sure about that?" Mac asked.

She propped her hands on her hips. "Why do you keep answering a question with a question?"

"I want to know more about you. What you're thinking, feeling, wishing for."

Now she was really in trouble. How long since it had been since anyone had cared about her in that way?

"And because your questions are all so foolish," he added.

They were, Erin thought indignantly, if his feelings were aboveboard and he could totally separate attraction and desire, and the process of closing a business deal. But if, as she half suspected, his emotions were as tangled as hers, they should run as far and fast from each other as they possibly could.

Unfortunately, she couldn't get a good reading from him, courtesy of his calm, inscrutable expression. "Look,

I just want to know why you kissed me." *I want to know,* she added silently to herself, *if it meant anything.*

The look in his eyes became even harder to decipher. "It was dark. You're pretty. You smelled good. And felt amazing. And," he finished huskily, "you tasted pretty nice, too. Like that cup of peppermint tea you'd been drinking, before I came back downstairs. And like, for lack of a better way of describing it, you."

He had tasted good, too. And felt so warm and strong and male. She hung on to her irritation with effort. "Gavin said the two of you spoke about us."

"Yeah." Mac let out a breath. "Your brother wasn't too happy he caught us making out."

Though Gavin was a year younger, he had taken on the role of her male protector in the family since their folks died. Just as Erin had assumed the role of mama bear. They acted as surrogate parents to the rest of the brood, which made their sibling relationship a lot more complicated.

Aware that the Prairie Natural Gas roughnecks were still watching her and Mac, Erin turned her back on the men. "I wasn't happy about it, either."

"The kissing?" Mac studied her. "Or getting caught?"

"Both."

He pursed his lips, clearly not believing her on the first, accepting the truth of the second.

Erin knew he had a point. Had Gavin not come downstairs, she and Mac could have ended the embrace in a more leisurely, natural way. Said whatever needed to be said then, instead of putting it off until now, when everything was so much more confused and complicated. Mainly because Mac had insisted on bringing his company's proposed wind farm and her land into the mix.

She held his gaze with effort. "I think you should know I am not interested in selling the ranch."

Reaching into his pocket, he withdrew the check for the boots and pressed it into her palm. "And I think you should try having an open mind. At least about a wind farm." He squeezed her fingers briefly, then smiled again and stepped away. "See you tonight."

Chapter Five

"There's no reason to be frowning," Bess told Erin, the moment the twins walked into the conference room at Travis Anderson's law office. "The meeting hasn't even started yet."

There was every reason, Erin thought, as she took a seat opposite her sisters. She didn't like feeling as if her life was spinning out of control again.

And it was, in ways she had never expected.

"I, for one, am anxious to hear what Mac has to say," Nicholas stated.

Gavin agreed. "Why don't we give the floor to him, so he can get right down to it?"

And get down to it he did.

For the next hour and a half, Mac gave all of them a crash course on wind power. What it could mean to the county, in terms of clean, renewable energy, and to them financially. He concluded by handing out a written offer to all five Monroe siblings.

Erin blinked at the multimillion-dollar sum. It was a lot of money for a ranch not suited for agricultural purposes. "Does this include the house and barns?"

"Yes. Although we could take them out, and a small plot of land they sit upon, but with 342 towers—each a hundred feet high—and the massive turbines atop them, we figured you probably wouldn't want to live there any longer."

"How noisy are they?" Bess asked.

"Each turbine makes the sound of a vehicle going seventy miles per hour," Mac explained.

Nicholas grimaced. "We'd have to get rid of our horses."

"Or stable them elsewhere," Mac said. "Perhaps at a new ranch?"

A thoughtful silence fell, and Erin eventually looked at the family attorney. "What do you think?"

Travis rocked back in his chair. "The offer is fair, when it comes to the price per acre. But you could also lease the land to NWE, and ask for an ongoing royalty, or percentage of the energy being generated and sold."

Mac frowned. "North Wind Energy would prefer to purchase the land outright."

"Once the wind farm is up and running, we won't want to live there," Gavin interjected.

"We're so far from town," Bridget added. "We're all eventually going to be living and working elsewhere, anyway."

"And I'm going off to college in two years," Nicholas reminded them.

Erin stared at her siblings. "So you *all* want to sell?"

"It would be sad to let the Triple Canyon Ranch go—especially the house—but it's time we were practical," Bess said gently. "Besides, you have to admit…it would be a lot easier on you to live closer to the store. In town, even."

"Obviously, you'd all have to agree," Travis interjected calmly. "And you need time to think about it, really consider, before you decide. I advise you to take a few weeks, at the very least."

Erin stared at her four siblings, hardly able to comprehend their attitude. They were all so unsentimental and matter-of-fact. "The Triple Canyon Ranch has been home to Monroes for four generations."

"All the more reason," Gavin concluded, "for us to finally be sensible and let it go."

"ARE YOU OKAY?" Travis asked Erin as Mac walked out with her siblings.

"I don't know," she murmured, still in shock. "This isn't just about the money."

Gavin walked back in. "You're right, Erin. It's about you. And the fact that you've sacrificed so much to carry on for Mom and Dad in their absence, seeing to it that Nicholas and the twins were able to live in the home where we all were born..."

"You wanted that, too." Erin helped Travis clean up the bottles of water and coffee cups and carry them to the law office break room.

"But I wasn't here for most of it," Gavin said. "I was off at med school, and now residency. I wasn't the one struggling to run the store and the ranch and make sure the taxes and the tuitions were paid. All the while weathering my own tragedies and raising my own family."

Erin stiffened. "I haven't minded."

Gavin sighed. "No one says you have. Just that it's time for you to move on. Comfortably."

Erin stared at her brother, blinking back unexpected tears. "But what about—"

A throat cleared, and she turned to see Mac looming in the doorway. "Sorry to interrupt. I forgot my briefcase. I wanted to get it before I headed over to the pizza restaurant to pick up Heather."

Erin glanced at her watch. "I've got to go get Sammy and Stevie, too."

She and Mac said their goodbyes, then walked out.

Just down the street, standing outside the Lone Star Dance Hall, were the roughnecks from Prairie Natural Gas. Cleaned up and ready for an evening out, they were looking Erin and Mac's way.

"You seem upset," Mac observed.

Crushed and depressed was more like it.

Erin shrugged, struggling to keep her feelings under wraps. "The meeting wasn't what I expected."

He sent her a searching glance. "The meeting or your family's reaction to my pitch?"

A mixture of anger and defiance warred within her. "The ranch means something to me."

He slid a hand beneath her elbow as they crossed the street. "It always will, whether you live there or not."

Erin jerked away from his touch. Behind them, she heard the rude hooting and hollering of the workmen. "How pragmatic."

"Realistic." Mac corrected with an implacable look. He shoved his hands in the pockets of his trousers as they continued down the sidewalk. "And I guess you're right. I am."

Erin came to a halt, several storefronts away from the pizza parlor. "How much of what Gavin said to me did you overhear?"

Mac's eyes darkened. "Pretty much all of it."

"Then you know." Erin tilted her head to one side. "You've got four votes in your pocket. All you have left to do is convince me, and you're right where you want to be." Without another word, she stalked off.

"SO HOW DID IT GO?" Mac's boss asked on the phone that evening.

Mac glanced over at his daughter, snuggled in her bed, sleeping soundly. With her favorite teddy bear cuddled in her arms, Heather looked so sweet and innocent. So young. It was hard to imagine Erin losing her daughter to cancer at the same age.

"Four of the five heirs are ready to sell," he said, forcing his mind back to business.

Louise made an approving sound. "I trust you'll be able to convince the fifth?"

Could he? Usually for Mac, situations like this were all about presenting the business proposal and closing the deal. Having Erin involved made it personal for him. He wasn't used to that. It felt, suddenly, as if his loyalties were divided. He wasn't used to that, either. "I'm working on it," he said finally.

"What about the county commissioners?"

"I ran the figures for them. They're slowly getting on board."

"And on the home front?" his boss probed. "Things settling down there?"

It was surprising how quickly his daughter had adapted. "Heather likes her new school. I should be able to stay in Texas until the project is approved, the contracts signed."

"That's what I want to hear."

"Once that happens," Mac warned, "I'm going to want to make some changes."

"I figured as much," Louise returned kindly. "You just let me know how NWE can better accommodate you. You're too valuable a member of the team for us to lose."

"Thanks." Mac hung up and went back to working on the agenda for the following day.

He was nearly done when he heard a ruckus outside. Pickup trucks arriving, a little too fast. Doors slamming. Rowdy, slurred voices. Hoots of laughter. *Great,* Mac thought, as the partying in the parking lot of the Laramie Inn picked up. This was all he needed, for Heather to wake up.

He was just putting on his shoes to go outside and ask the guys to tone it down when a vehicle alarm went off. The piercing sound echoed through the parking lot.

Mac looked through the drapes to see whose vehicle it was, and discovered the blinking lights and honking horn were from his rented SUV.

Super. He cast another look at Heather, grateful she was still asleep. He grabbed his keys and eased out of the hotel room onto the cement balcony of the second floor. He hit the panic button on the keypad. Nothing. The alarm kept ringing instead of deactivating.

Frowning, Mac headed down the outside stairs. When he reached his SUV, a menacing figure stepped out of the shadows. Mac recognized the tall, bearded man from the group of roughnecks who had been following him around. The guy had a transmitter in his hand, and he punched it with his thumb. Mac's car fell silent, the way it should have when he hit his own keypad.

Mac swore silently. The scoundrels had tampered with the rented vehicle's security system. It didn't matter how. They'd done it, and they wanted him to know they were responsible.

His opponent removed a ball-peen hammer from his belt. "This vehicle of yours is a damn nuisance."

Mac looked his opponent in the eye. "I don't want any trouble here."

His adversary sneered. "If you felt that way, should

have stayed back East, city boy." He smashed in a tail-light with the hammer.

Another roughneck, reeking of booze, stepped out from behind a car. He cradled a tire iron in his hands. "And just so you know we mean business, Philadelphia…" he taunted, rearing back to smash first one SUV headlamp, then the other.

Aware that everything they had done so far could easily be pleaded down to misdemeanors, Mac adapted a bored tone and said, "Why don't you-all just move along, and we'll chalk it up to one too many whiskeys on a wild Friday night."

"You-all hear that, fellows?" A third man emerged from the shadows. "This dude is trying to talk just like us!"

A fourth instigator came around to the left of Mac, a knife in his palm. "Well, gotta reward that, boys!" He slashed one front tire, then the next.

"You do know this is a *rental* car?" Mac asked drily.

"So we're not hurting you, is that it?"

He returned the intimidating taunt of the gang leader with a lethal glare of his own. "Pretty much."

"Then maybe—" the second troublemaker stepped forward "—we should rectify that."

Mac scoffed. "I'll take you all on, but it's got to be fair. Fists only."

"One of you? Against all four of us?"

"Unless," Mac dared, "you're all so scared of me you *have* to use a weapon?"

THE PHONE CALL CAME at four in the morning. Caller ID said Laramie Community Hospital. Grateful all her family were home and accounted for except her oldest brother—who was working the night shift—Erin grabbed for the phone. "Hello," she said sleepily.

"Erin? It's Gavin. We've got a problem here."

She sat up against the headboard, rubbing the sleep from her eyes. Over the phone, she was pretty sure she could hear a child crying. It sounded like a little girl.

"Mac Wheeler was brought in. He's getting stitched up now."

Stitched up? Erin blinked, wide awake. "What about Heather?"

"That's her you hear crying. Uh—she's pretty upset, and none of the staff can calm her down. Mac said you're really the only one she's bonded with locally, so far."

Erin's pulse quickened in alarm. "I'll be right there."

She threw on some clothes and then went in to tell the twins where she was going. They promised to hold down the fort in her absence. Two minutes later, Erin was on the road. Although she tried not to imagine the worst, her heart raced the entire way there.

Finally, she reached the hospital and parked in the lot. Gavin saw her the moment she rushed through the E.R. doors. He waved her past the front desk and led her toward an exam room.

Heather was still crying, though much more softly. "Is Mac…" Erin couldn't finish the sentence.

Her brother lifted a hand. "He's going to be fine. Just got beat up a little. They had to wake Heather up when they were trying to get him to the hospital. She saw the blood and the black eye and got scared."

"Black eye?"

Gavin put a hand on Erin's shoulder and propelled her toward the door. "Just go in and tell her everything is going to be okay. And when she's calm, you can go see Mac. Okay? No one knows how to make a child stop crying better than you."

For good reason, Erin thought. She'd had tons of practice when her own little girl was sick.

Erin slowly walked through the door. The nurse attempting to comfort Heather slipped out, leaving them alone. "Hey, Heather, how are you doing?" Erin dropped her bag and went toward the child, both arms open.

The little girl fell into them, still sobbing, and clung tightly. Erin's own eyes filled. Struggling not to sob herself, she sat down and shifted Heather onto her lap. Wrapping both arms around her, Erin cradled her close. Murmuring softly, she rocked back and forth. "Hey, now, hey, it's okay. It's okay, honey. I'm here, and your daddy is going to be fine."

Heather's tears drenched Erin's chest, and she held on to her with a death grip. "The bad mans h-h-hit Daddy."

Bad mans? Plural? Erin gulped, and spoke even more calmly. "Did you see it?"

"The doctor guys in the fire truck said so."

So Heather had heard the EMS team talking.

Not cool.

But perhaps, under the circumstances, unavoidable. Erin stroked Heather's tangled blond curls with one hand and, still rocking her gently, patted her back with the other. "Were the policemen there?"

"Yes. They t-t-took the bad men away."

Thank heavens! "Then everything really is going to be okay," Erin assured her, "if the bad men are all gone."

She stroked a hand down Heather's spine, aware that the child had stopped crying and was beginning to relax. "I know you were scared," she soothed. "But even so, you've been very brave tonight, Heather."

The child shuddered in relief and closed her eyes.

Her heart aching at the thought of all the little girl had been through, Erin continued rocking her. Minutes later, Heather was sound asleep.

A nurse eased in. "Good work."

"Thanks."

The woman took Heather's pulse. Together, they eased the girl onto the bed, where she lay down against the pillows, her eyes closed, her teddy snuggled in her arms.

"I'll stay with her until you get back," the nurse promised. "Her dad is ready to be released."

MAC KNEW ERIN WAS on the premises. He'd recognized her sweet, feminine voice the moment she entered the E.R. But nothing prepared him for the impact of seeing her walk into the exam room in jeans, a snug-fitting T-shirt and boots. With her curls tousled in that just-out-of-bed way, her stance kick-butt Texan, she looked like the heroine in a big-screen movie, come to save the day.

Worried green eyes roved over him for a long, heart-stealing moment. She exhaled so deeply her breasts rose and fell, then she shook her head. "At least tell me the other guys look worse." Her soft, bare lips curved slightly as she sashayed nearer.

For once, Mac didn't rush to rise as a lady entered the room. He lay on the stretcher, one hand folded behind his throbbing head. Needing to hold on to something, he caught her hand in his.

Unlike the last time they'd seen each other, she made no move to pull away.

Their eyes met. Held. Emotion and the sparks of something more elemental arced between them.

He'd never been more grateful to see a woman in his life, even if he hadn't a clue what to say to her. "You heard, hmm?"

Still holding his palm, Erin sat down on the gurney beside him, her hip resting lightly against his. Her gaze drifted over his face. "Heather's version. That there were 'multiple mans' hitting you."

Mac started to smile, then grimaced. "Sad but true." Damned if every inch of his face and upper body didn't ache like a son of a bitch.

Still looking deep into his eyes, Erin lifted her eyebrows. "Should I ask why?"

Mac gave an abridged version of what had happened.

She sighed loudly, shook her head. "You really thought it was a good idea to taunt them that way?"

Never one to second-guess himself, especially in the heat of battle, Mac shrugged. "I wanted them to put their weapons down."

Erin tightened her grasp on his hand. "It didn't occur to you that four guys pounding on you at once was not your best option?"

"That wasn't part of the plan. The sheriff's deputies arriving just in time to keep me from getting a few broken ribs and a busted kidney, however, was."

Erin bent closer, in a drift of lilac. She examined the cut just below his lip, the stitches along his temple, the others on the underside of his chin. "So they limited their boxing to your face?"

Mac nodded. He pushed the sheet away and struggled to sit up. "Pretty much, except for the few blows they landed in my gut."

Placing soft hands on his shoulder and spine, Erin assisted him. "Yikes." She reared back. "That's a helluva bruise, Mac!" She ran her fingers over his chest. "And another one here!" She touched his left pec. "You sure you're okay?"

"Yes." He reached for his bloodstained shirt and shrugged it on with her help. "Stop fussing."

She pushed his clumsy hands aside and finished buttoning the front. "Not in my nature." She looked around, found his jeans and loafers. Handed them over.

Mac threw his legs over the edge of the gurney and sat there, belatedly realizing he still felt a little woozy. Not surprising, since he'd nearly had the stuffing beaten out of him by four idiots.

Concerned, Erin moved to help him with his slacks, too.

Trying not to think about her exquisitely gently touch as she guided his legs into his clothes, Mac closed his eyes, glad he was too weak to get a hard-on. Or was he? Damn.

He pushed her away before she could discover what was going on, and then motioned for her to turn around.

Her cheeks flushing with color, she complied.

Mac struggled into his pants, fastened them and pulled down his shirttail. Planting a hand on the table, he stood and shoved his feet into his shoes. "You were awfully good with Heather just now."

Erin turned back around, a hint of a smile tugging her lips. "How do you know?"

Mac shrugged and picked up the ice pack they'd given him to put against his swollen eye. "Exam room walls are pretty thin. Plus I had them leave my door open, so I'd be able to monitor things while they finished stitching me up. I would have had Heather in here with me, but…"

"Having her see the needles probably wasn't the best idea under the circumstances."

"No, but neither was having her in the next room, crying her eyes out, either." Mac straightened, then waited a minute for the spinning to recede.

Erin moved closer. Before he could say anything, she had a steadying hand beneath his elbow. "So what next?" she murmured.

Mac swallowed. He'd tried not to think about the fact that he'd unwittingly put his child in harm's way by bringing her here with him. "Heather and I need a ride to wherever."

He couldn't see going back to the Laramie Inn.

Not tonight, anyway.

His daughter would freak.

"You're coming home with me," Erin said firmly.

Mac didn't want to put her and her family in danger, either.

She saw his reservation but brushed it off. "Listen to me, Mac. I'm not hearing any arguments. The Laramie County Sheriff's Department is excellent and has everything under control."

That part was true, Mac knew. After the altercation, they'd quickly restored order. Too bad he hadn't called them at the outset, when he'd first noticed the roughnecks following him around.

"You and Heather have both been through enough. You'll come home with me," Erin insisted, "and get some sleep and food. Then you can figure out where to go from there."

Chapter Six

"Mac?" A delicate voice infiltrated the hazy cocoon surrounding him. Footsteps neared, followed by the faint scent of lilac. He felt a shift of the mattress, the warmth of a hovering body and a silky hand on his forearm. "I hate to wake you, but…"

Mac blinked, opened his eyes. Erin was sitting next to him on the trundle bed in the sun-washed bedroom. In a powder-blue T-shirt and knee-length khaki shorts, she looked pretty and relaxed.

And, Mac noted, all business. "Deputy Rio Vasquez is here to take a statement from you."

And here he'd thought she had come in to see him. He rubbed his eyes, then winced, realizing his scraped knuckles were as tender and achy as the rest of him. "What time is it?" he asked groggily.

"Almost noon."

Which meant he'd been asleep about six hours. Mac drew in a deep breath, found the muscles around his ribs hurt, too. He rubbed at his stiff, painful shoulder. "Where's Heather?"

Smiling reassuringly, Erin inclined her head toward the window. "In the driveway, playing street hockey with Sammy and Stevie."

"How's she doing?" he rasped, remembering how his daughter had sobbed when she discovered he'd been hurt.

Erin's smile widened even more. "Great. She woke up around eight, came down and had a big breakfast with the boys, then went outside to play."

Mac studied Erin's soft maternal glow. "No more tears?"

Erin shook her head in wonder. "Surprising, isn't it?" She reached over and briefly squeezed his forearm, before settling back and clasping her hands around one knee. "But kids are remarkably resilient, especially when they feel safe."

Mac could see how that would've happened, despite the trauma they'd been through the night before. Hell, even he felt safe with Erin beside him. "Everything else okay?" he asked, not really wanting to move from the cozy bed just yet. Not when she was sitting here beside him, looking like an angel of mercy.

He searched her face, seeing none of the anxiety she'd exhibited the night before when she'd gotten her first look at him. "How are you feeling?"

"Just fine." She gave his forearm another friendly pat and stood. "You want me to tell Deputy Vasquez you'll be right down?"

Mac nodded. He needed to splash some water on his face, brush his teeth, wake up a little more.

A few minutes later, he met them in the living room.

As Rio Vasquez took his statement, the color drained from Erin's face. Too late, Mac realized this was the first time she had heard the un-sugarcoated version.

"What's going to happen to the men who did this?" she asked, wringing her hands anxiously.

Rio packed up his laptop computer. "There are outstanding warrants for all four of them in Oklahoma for a similar situation. So as soon as they're arraigned this afternoon, they'll be transferred to a jail there, where they'll be held without bail until the trial, which, frankly, could be months from now."

Erin breathed a sigh of relief.

Mac thanked Rio and walked him to the door.

The twins, hearing Mac was up, left their studying long enough to come downstairs to view the damage. "Wow, Gavin wasn't kidding when he said you got the stuffing beat out of you," Bridget teased, examining the damage like the nursing student she was.

"Nice job on the stitches, though. I doubt you'll have much of a scar," Bess said, examining his temple and the underside of his chin.

"Just enough to add a dangerously male aura." Bridget winked.

Erin glared at the three of them. "It's not funny."

Mac smiled, feeling slightly better, now that he'd been up awhile. "It is a little."

Erin made a face at him, unconvinced.

To Mac's surprise, the pilgrimage continued throughout the early afternoon.

The kids briefly stopped playing long enough to come in and have lunch with Mac. They presented him with Spider-Man Band-Aids. "Your stitches will look way cooler that way."

"Thanks, guys." With Erin's assistance, Mac gamely put them on over the ones the hospital nurses had already placed.

The children grinned, happy to have helped, then asked a lot of questions about the assault. Mac assured them it wasn't really a big deal—the men had just had too much to drink and weren't thinking straight; they had surely learned their lesson now.

Travis Anderson stopped by next, to see what he could do.

He was followed by the director of the Montessori school where Heather had just enrolled.

The Laramie Inn manager brought a fruit basket, and some pastries from the local German bakery.

The rental car agency assured Mac that the insurance company would cover the damages to the SUV, and then they dropped off a brand-new one for him to drive.

Next, a few county commissioners arrived. "We want you to know we've put the Prairie Natural Gas company on notice," one of them told Mac. "This kind of behavior won't be tolerated."

"Did they admit to sending the men after Mac?" Erin asked.

The commissioner shook his head. "But if we find any link whatsoever to the mugging, they'll be fired as suppliers and out of the running for the power-plant expansion."

Erin nodded. "That seems right."

"It doesn't mean you and your company have won the bid by any means," the other commissioner told Mac, "but given what happened, and the courageous way you handled yourself, the people of Laramie are a lot more willing to listen to you."

"Whoever would've thought," Mac murmured to Erin, after everyone had left, "that getting mugged would give me an automatic in here in Laramie County?"

Erin walked into the kitchen, with Mac on her heels. She slipped on a pair of oven mitts and took two large baking dishes filled with roasting chicken from the oven. While he watched, she brushed barbecue sauce onto the sizzling golden pieces. A delicious aroma filled the room.

"It's not the getting beat up part, it's the courage you

showed." Finished, she slid the pans back into the oven, then turned to him. "You were clearly outnumbered, and outarmed, yet you stood up to those four thugs until the sheriff arrived."

Mac shrugged. "Not such a big deal, given the collective sum of their intelligence."

She grinned at his joke, then walked closer to inspect his scraped knuckles and the bruises on his hands and face. She tenderly brushed a hand across his cheek. "Where did you learn to fight like that?"

In the past, Mac had found there was no point in trying to pretend his background was anything but blue-collar. He wouldn't do it now. He caught her hand and pressed it against the center of his chest. "I grew up in south Philly. It wasn't the kindest, gentlest neighborhood."

Briefly, she leaned into his touch. "Couldn't your parents protect you?"

Mac exhaled. Usually, he didn't like talking about himself, especially with someone who—prior to his beating, anyway—had been on the opposite side of a business equation.

"When my mom knew about it, sure." Although Mac tried to keep his guard up, Erin's coaxing smile somehow drew the next confession out of him. "Usually, I didn't tell her."

"What about your father?" she asked softly.

Their eyes met, and it was as if she suddenly realized they were standing way too close, because she extricated her fingers from his and moved away.

"My dad died in a factory accident when I was eight."

Her expression changed. "I'm sorry," she said compassionately, looking at him as if she wanted him to go on.

Surprising himself, Mac did. "The situation made me tougher than I probably would have been. My mom was a hotel maid. I saw how hard she had to work with so little education. It made me determined to achieve more." He had wanted to give her a better life, and for a while, he had.

Erin smiled again. "She must be very proud of you."

"She was, until she died. Eight years ago from emphysema."

Erin reached out and squeezed his hand briefly. "I'm sorry. I know what it is to lose your parents."

Mac felt a punch to the gut at the memory. "It sucks, doesn't it?"

She nodded. Their eyes locked and he felt the connection between them deepen. Which really sucked, because eventually they'd have to get back to business, and instinct told him Erin wasn't going to want the wind farm situated on the Triple Canyon Ranch tomorrow, any more than she had last night. And without all five Monroe heirs on board, a deal wasn't happening.

Which meant, Mac thought ruefully, he had his work cut out for him. He stepped back and adapted the easiest tone he could manage. "So...do you think the visitors are going to keep coming, or are we done for now?"

Erin's eyes lit with humor. "Probably done. Which is a good thing, because dinner's ready, and it's time to call the kids."

She had just reached the front of the house when the sound of a car engine rumbled closer.

Erin went to the window, looked out. Fingertips pressed to her forehead, she let out a low moan.

"Who is it?" Mac asked.

She sighed. Loudly. "My ex-husband."

TALK ABOUT LOUSY TIMING, Erin thought, as G.W. climbed out of his pickup truck emblazoned with the words Horizon Oil Company.

Sammy and Stevie whooped with joy at the sight of their father, and ran toward him, arms outstretched. "Dad! What are you doing here! How long can you stay? Did you miss us? We missed you!"

And on it went.

Watching, Erin struggled against her own resentment—and relief, that he had finally shown up again. Albeit unannounced. Her boys needed their dad, now more than ever.

If only G.W. would accept that, and do more.

But knowing him, occasional stop-bys were the best she could reasonably expect.

G.W. showed up when he felt like it.

And was absent when he didn't.

Fortunately, her boys had come to know that about their dad, and they loved him anyway.

Erin waited for the boys to finish greeting their dad and introducing their new friend, Heather.

"Her daddy is Mr. Wheeler," Sammy explained, pointing to Mac, who'd come to stand next to Erin on the porch.

He extended his hand. "Call me Mac."

G.W. looked him up and down before focusing on his face. "That's some shiner you've got there. Nice Band-Aids, too."

Mac grinned. "Sammy and Stevie gave them to me."

G.W. patted them both on the back. "That's my boys for you. Hearts of gold!"

Erin smiled. "Would you like to stay for dinner, G.W.? It's ready."

"Thanks." Her ex-husband removed his hat and ran his fingers through his sandy hair. "Yeah. I would."

She looked at the children. "Wash up, okay?"

Sammy, Stevie and Heather raced to comply. G.W.

inhaled the aroma coming from the doorway and swaggered up the steps to stand between Erin and Mac on the porch. "Oven-barbecued chicken?" He stood with his back to Mac.

With a droll look on his face, Mac stepped politely aside to give her ex room.

Erin had to work not to roll her eyes in exasperation. The last thing she needed to do was egg G.W. on. "You guessed it."

"Looks like I timed it just right tonight." He looked over his shoulder at Mac. "Always was one of my favorites."

Was it her imagination, Erin wondered, or was G.W. acting a little territorial? Of course, maybe that wasn't so surprising. This had once been his home.

Bess and Bridget came downstairs about the same time that Nicholas came in the front door. They all greeted their former brother-in-law coolly and politely.

Erin knew with G.W. on the premises they'd prefer to back out of dinner. For her sake, they stayed.

Fortunately, the meal was dominated by conversation with the kids. Only after they'd finished and asked to be excused, to play outdoors some more before dark, did the talk turn to more complicated adult matters.

"So tell me about this wind farm your company is proposing," G.W. said from his old place at the head of the long table.

Mac explained the basics while dishes were cleared, coffee cups brought out.

Nicholas added eagerly, "It's clean, renewable energy that produces no greenhouse gases or other pollutants."

"Horizon Oil has recently developed some new, more environmentally friendly technology, too," G.W. said. He got up to help himself to a second plate of peach cobbler. "In fact, our geologists think there might be oil beneath some of the ridges that line the three canyons here on the ranch. We're interested in a lease for the mineral rights."

Erin, whose own appetite had faded the moment her ex had shown up, looked at G.W. He knew damn well how she felt about this. "You're kidding."

He was not.

G.W. shrugged. "It's not like you're using the land for anything else. If we strike oil, you'd be rich. If not, you could still sell to the wind-farm company later."

Bridget looked at Mac, who'd been watching G.W. make his pitch. "Is that true?" she asked.

Mac drained the last of his coffee. "No. The county commissioners are going to decide on the method for solving the energy shortage in the next few weeks. They'll either expand the current natural gas plant to provide more kilowatt hours to residents, or switch to an alternate method—like wind power—to boost the current system."

G.W. shook his head. "I can't see them cluttering up the landscape with hundreds of huge wind turbines."

"As opposed to putting in drilling rigs and heavy equipment?" Erin couldn't help but retort.

G.W. sent her an accusing look. "You always did resent my devotion to my work."

That was unfair. Unable to help herself, Erin snapped, "When it kept you from our daughter's bedside, you're darn right, I did."

A tense silence fell. Everyone but she and G.W. were looking at their plates.

Finally, he cleared his throat. "Well, I can see you're going to need time to think about this." He finished the rest of his dessert in a single gulp and stood, glancing out the kitchen window at the kids. They were playing on the backyard swing set and fort, in plain view.

Then, in a scene that was heartrendingly familiar, he headed in the opposite direction, toward the front door.

Erin scraped back her chair. Once again, her ex had left her no choice but to chase after him. "You're leaving?"

G.W. grabbed his hat off the coatrack and placed it on his head. "I need to be in Corpus Christi by tomorrow afternoon."

"The boys…"

G.W. brought the brim down over his eyes. "Will understand."

Would they? Erin wondered, hurt, despite herself.

G.W. fished his keys out of his pocket and strode toward his pickup truck. Clenching her teeth, she followed him down the steps. "At least say goodbye to them."

He kept right on going. "Why don't you do that for me? You know how messy it was the last time."

Every time.

He called over his shoulder, "Just tell them I'll be back in a few days, when I bring you the papers to sign."

"HE LEFT AGAIN?" Nicholas asked when Erin walked back into the kitchen. "Without telling the kids?"

It was bad, Erin thought, when even a sixteen-year-old knew the quick getaway was wrong. She swallowed around the ache in her throat. Damn G.W. and his devotion to business.

Too embarrassed to look at their dinner guest and see what he thought, Erin turned her attention to the task of loading the dishwasher. "He said he'll be back in a few days with papers for me to sign."

Her siblings scoffed in unison. "G.W. really doesn't know you at all, does he?" Bridget spat out.

The truth was, he never had.

And maybe, Erin thought, she had never known her

ex, either, because this behavior still surprised her. Every time. She kept hoping he would do the right thing. And kept right on being disappointed.

The twins stepped in, the way good sisters did. "How about we take the kids into town to see the new animated movie?" Bess said.

Bridget added, "I know it's a little late, but it's not a school night and it would probably be a good distraction."

"I'll go, too," Nicholas volunteered.

Which would make three chaperones for three kids. "It's okay with me," Mac said.

Erin sighed. Truth was, she could use a little time to herself.

Luckily, the boys were as happy to go as they were disappointed to find out that G.W. had taken off, without warning, yet again.

Promising to be back by ten o'clock, the group left. Mac and Erin went back inside. "Why don't you let me do the dishes?" Mac suggested.

"You look like you ought to be in bed."

A low chuckle emanated from his broad chest.

Erin flushed. "You know what I mean. *Resting.*"

His eyes lit with a mischief. "Resting is the last thing I feel like doing."

Erin caught her breath. Desire, hot and potent, shifted through her. "Mac..." *Please don't make me want you. Please. Don't make me lose control.*

But he would, and he did. Cupping her shoulders with his big hands, he looked at her expectantly. "Give me one good reason why I shouldn't kiss you again," he murmured. "And I won't."

Chapter Seven

For both their sakes—for the sakes of everyone involved—Erin tried valiantly to come up with a reason not to get any closer to this big, strapping man. But all she could think about as Mac engulfed her in his arms was how much she wanted to kiss him.

Shoving caution aside, she went up on tiptoe. Mac's arms wrapped tightly around her middle, lifting her, until their hearts were beating in tandem. Slowly, inevitably, he lowered his lips to hers.

Erin caught her breath at the connection, and then the whole world seemed to stop. He tasted so good, so uniquely Mac. Everything about him was masculine and hard, completely inflexible and unyielding, and she reveled in the strength of his demand.

He was consumed with passion.

And heaven help them both, so was she.

Erin moaned, shifting her body higher, deepening the kiss. With a low groan, he welcomed the thrust and parry of her tongue sliding across his.

Emboldened, she nibbled on his lower lip, then the corners, licked her way across the top. And then the tables turned again. Mac lifted her all the way off the floor, pulling her up, spreading her legs with his palms, until her calves wrapped around his back and her thighs straddled his waist.

He cleared a path with one hand and set her on the kitchen counter. Stepped into the apex of her thighs. Hands threaded in her hair, he cupped her face and kissed her—deeper and deeper, barreling past her defenses, knocking down walls that had been up for way too long. Her heart racing, Erin met him stroke for stroke. The next thing she knew his hands were inching beneath her T-shirt, caressing her skin, moving ever upward.

Shocked, she sucked in an aroused breath as his palms covered her breasts, their heat and the stroking of his fingertips sending lightning zipping through her.

Erin broke off the kiss. "Mac..."

He rubbed a hand up her back, letting it settle at the nape of her neck. "Tell me to stop."

"I can't. You know I can't." Even if this was only physical, she wanted it. She wanted him.

He met her gaze. "Then...?"

"Let's go to my bed."

He kissed her again, long and hard and deep. Kissed her until she was shaking. "You're sure?" he whispered.

Erin knew if they went upstairs there'd be no stopping this runaway train they were on. She kissed the corner of his mouth. "I'm sure. Life is so short, Mac." For too long, she'd only been half living it. Who knew if this chance would come again?

"Can't argue with you there," Mac said gruffly, reminding her that he had suffered his own share of heartache and loss. And maybe been alone too long.

Hooking his hands around her hips, he pulled her toward him. He kissed her like he meant business, until every inch of her burned with need. Erin moaned and clamped her legs tighter around his waist. She was wet and trembling as he carried her, kissing her all the while, to the stairs.

Up them. Down the hall. With their lips still fused together, they made it to her bedroom. He had never been in there, she realized, as he slowly set her down next to the bed.

It was a feminine haven, the kind of abode she never could have had when she was married. An antique four-poster mahogany bed. Silk pink-and-white wallpaper. Flowered duvet and shams. A closet to die for and a chaise longue for reading.

Mac smiled as he glanced around. "It's perfect for you."

You're perfect for me, Erin thought, then wondered where that notion had come from. Impatient to take up where they'd left off, she hooked her hand in his belt, then rose on tiptoe again and kissed him fervently as she played with the top button on his slacks, her fingers brushing against the warm muscles of his abs. "Too much talking."

His hands skimmed beneath her T-shirt, over her ribs, to the undersides of her breasts. His thumbs rasped her hardened nipples. "Ah, but talking is what makes this memorable." He skimmed off her shirt, then her bra. Eyes darkening, he savored the sight of her.

Erin quivered. "I prefer touch." To demonstrate, she undid his zipper and moved her hand south. He was hot. Aroused. And so big.

She wasn't the only one who caught her breath. Mac groaned, moving against her. "Touch is nice." He undid her shorts, hooked his hands in the elastic and eased everything off.

"I told you." She sighed and kissed him back as he stroked her flesh.

"But so is letting you know just how beautiful you are." He slid a finger into her until she writhed helplessly against him.

"Mac…" Shaking, she withdrew long enough to get him naked, too. He was so magnificent, so fiercely male, she could barely look away from him. When he brought her against him again, she couldn't catch her breath.

"Like that, do you?" He kissed her deeply.

She arched against him, clinging to him like a lifeline. She had never felt pleasure this intense. He was hard and huge, his body rippling with sheer power. "Very much."

"Let's see how you feel about this." He stretched out over her on the bed. Pinned her hands on either side of her head and kissed his way down her neck. Across her collarbone. To her breasts.

He suckled gently, bringing her body to fierce pleasure, until she could take no more. "Mac…"

"Tell me what else you want."

Love from someone like you, she thought wistfully. *And tenderness. And hope for the future again. So that there will be more to my life than just holding on to what I've already got.*

But that wasn't what he was talking about, she knew. "For you to touch me…" she whispered, guiding his fingers.

"Here?" He stroked her.

"Mmm." Erin arched.

"And here?"

He caressed her with just the right rhythm, moving inside, paving the way, until dampness was flowing.

Erin shifted. "I want to touch you, too."

He pulled her back. "Later." Holding her captive, he moved lower still. His mouth took over where his fingers left off, sending her soaring, until at last she cried out, shuddered, held him close. "I want you."

He groaned and hugged her to him, his eyes fierce. "I want you, too. So much."

And then there was nothing but pleasure. Lifting her up, opening her, making them one. Together, they sailed ever higher, until there was only this moment in time, this chance to feel really and truly alive.

"NOT TOO SHABBY, HMM?" Mac teased, as their shudders slowly subsided and contentment took over. Wary of his weight, he shifted onto his back, with Erin still clasped to his chest.

She sucked in a breath. "Definitely not shabby." She buried her face in the crook of his neck. After a moment, she made a strangled sound of dismay. "And maybe not all that wise, either."

Here it came...the second thoughts. Mac stroked his hand through her hair. All he wanted was to make love to her again. Yet the instinctual part of him knew that this was as unusual an occurrence for Erin as it was for him.

He always thought first, acted later. Never let passion get him off course.

But passion was what had landed him here in the bed of the smartest, kindest woman he had ever met. In the midst of a pending business deal, no less. He stroked his hand through her soft, honey-blond curls, aware that their coupling was the only sane thing in a world suddenly gone a little crazy. "We don't have to analyze it, Erin." At least not now.

She rose on her elbows, looking tousled, and a little bit grumpy. "Spoken like a true traveling man."

"Don't compare me to your ex-husband."

Her pretty eyes narrowed. "Why not? In this respect you're the same."

She was trying to start a fight…to avoid dealing with this. He was close to giving in. Until he saw, by the look in her eyes, just how vulnerable she was. And knew to get sucked into that would be to lose her forever.

Mac loosened his hold on her. Watched as she sat up, clutched the sheet to her chest and pulled away. He folded his arms behind his head. "How would you have this play out, in a best-case scenario?"

Erin stood and, careful to keep the sheet wrapped around her, wandered through the dark room to collect her scattered clothing. "I'd appreciate it for what it was. Is."

Resentment built inside him. The one thing he detested most of all was a lack of honesty. "And what is that?"

"A perfect storm of mutual loneliness and physical need. One that needn't ever happen again."

Without another word, she stepped into the bathroom and partially shut the door. Mac stayed where he was, wishing he could watch her, forcing himself to allow her the privacy she desired.

Erin walked back out, fully dressed, hairbrush in hand. Without meeting his eyes, she positioned herself in front of her antique, full-length mirror and fixed her hair in the light streaming from the open bathroom door.

Mac sensed she wanted to force him out, so this evening could end badly, as she needed it to. Abruptly as dog-tired as he deserved to be, given everything that had happened in the past twenty-four hours, he rose and began to dress. There were times when a guy had to follow his instincts and go against the grain. This was one of them.

Pivoting, Erin lounged against the bureau and watched

him with narrowed eyes. "Don't you have anything to say?" she asked eventually.

Mac had suppressed enough feelings with his late wife to last him a lifetime. The last thing he wanted was another relationship where decorum and expectation trumped gut-level needs every time. "You want to know what I think?" he repeated. "I think, try as you might, you can't un-ring a bell. But if it'll make you happy to pretend we don't know how great it was to make love with each other—" he shrugged and moved away from her "—then do what you have to do."

Erin blinked. "And that's it?"

Mac noticed she looked stunned and hurt, but no more ready to admit their tryst was a good thing. "I want you, Erin," he told her wearily. "Not just as a sometime bedmate, but as my woman." He paused to look into her eyes. "But I'm not going to pressure you into anything. So for this to happen again, for anything to happen again, you're going to have to come to me."

SUNDAY MORNING, all three children walked into Erin's studio behind the garage, where she was busy cutting the leather for Mac's boots. Sammy took the lead. "Mom, Heather needs cowgirl boots and jeans. 'Cause we want to take her riding and she can't go unless she has that stuff to wear."

"Also," Stevie added importantly, before Erin had a chance to respond, "she's a little scared, because she's never been on a horse before. But she really, really wants to learn."

Heather, who was flanked by the boys, nodded emphatically.

Erin put down her cutting tools. "Have you talked to Heather's daddy?"

All three shook their heads. "But it'll be okay if you tell him it's okay," Stevie said.

Not so sure about that, Erin switched off the lamp above her worktable. "Let's go see, shall we?"

Mac was seated at the dining room table, working on his laptop computer. He was wearing khaki trousers and a yellow button-up shirt with the sleeves rolled up. His hair was rumpled, as if he'd forgotten to brush it when he got up that morning, but his face was clean-shaven. Two new Batman Band-Aids covered the stitches there. His bruises were more pronounced than the day before, but attractive in a rakish sort of way.

All in all, he looked sexy and at ease, and seeing him that way reminded Erin all over again how great it had been to make love with him the evening before.

"The kids have a question for you."

"Heather wants to ride a horse," Stevie said.

"And we want her to," Sammy added.

Mac looked at Erin with a lifted brow.

"It's okay with me if it's okay with you, but she says she's never ridden before," Erin told him.

"She hasn't."

"Have you?"

He smiled that wicked, teasing smile reminiscent of the day they'd met. "Only one way to find out," he said.

Which wasn't an answer. Yet it was, if flirting with her was an answer.

"We could go this afternoon if we outfit her with the proper gear," Erin suggested.

Mac was already on his feet. "Let's do it."

Monroe's didn't open on Sundays, which made the task easy and private. Erin unlocked the back door and led the way in. To avoid having to turn customers away, she left the front lights off. They went to the children's section. She consulted Heather on colors, then carried appropriate-size jeans and long-sleeved snap-front Western shirts to a dressing room.

Heather liked the regular-fit boot-cut jeans. She picked out a green-and-blue-plaid shirt. Mac talked her into getting a red gingham one, too, as well as another pair of jeans. Then it was off to the children's boot section.

Erin measured Heather's foot, then walked her over to view the rainbow of choices and designs. After much deliberation, Mac's little girl chose a medium brown, stack-heeled boot emblazoned with yellow and red flowers.

"You sure you don't want pink or lavender boots?" Mac asked, no doubt thinking about the color of her many outfits.

Heather shook her head. "No, Daddy. No more pink," she said firmly.

"She's gonna need a hat, too," Sammy said, coming over with a straw one that was just her size.

Heather put it on, checked out her reflection in the mirror and pirouetted with a smile. "Look, everybody, I'm a real cowgirl now!"

She sure was.

It turned out Mac needed riding clothes, too. While the kids went over to the children's play area in the corner of the store, Erin helped him find the right-size Wranglers and, at his request, a couple of snap-front shirts and a summer-weight Resistol to keep the sun out of his eyes.

She leaned against the wall outside the dressing room, eyes shut against the mental image of him changing, and the memories that evoked. "Need anything?" she asked.

The silence that fell seemed rife with double entendres.

Mac cleared his throat. "No. These are good."

A second later, when he stepped out, she found out how good. No question, he filled out a pair of Wranglers in a way that would make another man weep with envy. Trim waist. Flat abs. Nice backside. Make that *really* nice backside, Erin amended silently, as she continued to check out the fit of the denim over his masculine frame. In front, well, she knew all too well what lay hidden behind his zipper fly.

Man, did she ever.

Erin flushed, then nodded at the hat still sitting on the dressing-room bench. "Let's check out how it fits."

Quirking his lips, Mac reached for the Resistol and slanted it over his brow.

And damned if the man didn't look like a Texas cowboy born and bred.

"SO WHAT DO YOU THINK?" Mac asked his daughter an hour later, as he lifted her into the saddle of one of the ranch's most beloved geldings and climbed on behind her.

Erin smiled in approval and waved.

"I like it, Daddy!" Heather declared, holding on to the saddle horn with both hands. She leaned back so her shoulders and spine rested against her daddy's broad chest. With one arm around her, the other on the reins, Mac sat there oozing confidence.

He did know how to ride, after all, Erin noted.

That was proved as the five of them set out, Erin bringing up the rear, her boys and their two horses taking the lead, over the well-worn riding trail that wound through the prettiest—and safest—terrain of the Triple Canyon Ranch.

"I'm beginning to see why you wouldn't want to give this up," Mac told Erin after a while, reining his horse in to keep pace with hers. "It's gorgeous out here, in a way that the aerial view doesn't show."

Erin inclined her head. "Bad for cattle."

"I can see that. Probably a little too rocky and arid." He waggled his brows earnestly. "Nice for a wind farm, though."

She rolled her eyes and sighed. "How did I know you were going to say that?" she asked, peering at him from beneath the brim of her hat.

"ESP?"

"Or a rancher's intuition."

A brief silence fell as they moved along. "How often do you ride?" Mac asked eventually.

Erin shrugged, pleased at the easy way Mac set the pace of his horse to hers. The two of them were riding with the same camaraderie as her boys.

"Not often enough these days. Between the commute to town for work and school, and homework and dinner and dishes and chores… We're lucky if we fit it in once a week. Worst-case scenario, once a month."

"That's a shame."

It was. Their horses needed more exercise.

"Was it ever any different?"

"Meaning when…" Aware that Heather was half listening to their conversation as she took in the scenery, Erin avoided saying Angelica's name. "Um…was alive?"

Heather turned her head. "You mean Angelica? Sammy and Stevie's little sister?"

So the boys had been confiding in a way that was not fraught with tears and pain. The knowledge was new to Erin. She had never known her sons to be able to open up like this. Aware that it was really helping them to have a "little sister" with them, even temporarily, she replied kindly, "Yes. I'm speaking about my little girl, the one who is in heaven now."

Heather nodded. "With my mommy."

"Yes," Mac said. "They're both in heaven."

Even though we wish they were still here. Erin swallowed around the sudden ache in her throat.

Heather looked up at the sky and studied the fluffy white clouds. "Do you think they know each other?"

Mac seemed at a loss.

Which left it up to Erin. "Well, now that you mention it…" Erin said thickly after a moment. "I think they just might be together right now, looking down and watching over us…keeping us safe."

Heather smiled at the image. Mac's eyes glistened, along with Erin's. And that was the last any of them said for a long time.

"THANKS FOR TODAY," Mac said, walking into Erin's studio much later.

She looked up from her sewing machine. "You're very welcome. We had fun, too. For the first time in an eternity, it felt like we were a family."

His eyes fell to the wrinkle she'd been putting in across the toe, which would allow his boot to bend as he moved. "Us, too."

Erin sat back in her chair and looked him in the eye. "Ever since…" She swallowed thickly and pushed on. "It's been like there was something missing in our lives."

Understanding filled his blue eyes. "It's like there's a hole in your heart you can't fill."

Erin nodded. "Anyway, it was good to let go of that for once. Just be in the moment and—I know it sounds a little corny—feel the love." Remember what it was to be a complete unit with a mom and a dad and kids, all having fun. Even if, technically, they weren't the same family.

Mac came closer. Like her, he had showered after their ride. He smelled amazing, like soap and aftershave lotion.

He pulled up a chair next to her, straddled it backward and rested his folded arms across the top. "Just so you know. I haven't taken your incredible hospitality for granted. I'm still looking for a place for us to rent, short-term."

Was that why he'd sought her out? To tell her he was leaving? Erin stiffened. "Please don't. Sammy and Stevie have missed their little sister. Having Heather here has helped them so much."

"It's helped us, too," Mac replied. "But…what about you?"

Erin jerked in a breath. "What do you mean?" She put the pieces of the left boot aside and reached for the pieces of the right.

He watched her sew another wrinkle. "Is it going to be awkward?"

Erin checked to make sure her stitches were correct. "Because we made love?"

He met her gaze without hesitation. "We can't pretend it didn't happen."

Or might again. Aware how much she wanted him now—just as she had all day—Erin finished stitching the top of the filigree and stood. "You're thinking of kissing me again, aren't you?"

He slid her a long look. "I said I wouldn't seduce you into anything you didn't want."

And he hadn't. Trouble was… Erin took a deep breath, deciding maybe it was time she was a little more forthright. "What if I've decided I might have been a tad hasty?"

He smiled seductively. "I'm open for anything."

"Really?" Aware she was trembling slightly, she took his hand and drew him to his feet.

He gave her a once-over that kicked her pulse into high gear. "Really."

"Then come here." Throwing caution aside, she drew him into her arms. "And let me find out if what we felt last night was as excellent as I remember."

Chapter Eight

Mac hadn't come to her studio intending to kiss her. But now that the offer was on the table, and it was her idea, he was all for it. Shifting her nearer, he lowered his head and claimed her mouth with his. Needing to feel close to her again, he moved his hips against hers and delivered a deep, demanding kiss, savoring the softness of her body and the sweet taste of her mouth until Erin and he were both breathless. And then he kissed her some more, taking everything she had to give, giving her everything in return.

They were both sighing in pleasure, wanting more, and Mac was about to let her go long enough to lock the door, when Gavin burst in.

"Erin? I— Whoa." He glowered at Mac. "Again?"

Embarrassed, Erin stumbled backward. Mac lifted a staying hand. "Before you go off half-cocked, Gavin, this was mutual."

"I can see that." Her brother swung around to Erin with narrowed eyes. "I thought you should know the kids are all still awake. They're up in the game room, with the lights off, watching some sort of kid comedy on TV and giggling like crazy. The boys tried to tell me they had permission from you, but since it's ten o'clock and tomorrow is a school day, I figured not."

"You figured right." Erin flushed. "I'll take care of it."

"I'll go with you," Mac offered.

The two of them hurriedly left the studio.

"You want to talk about this?" he asked as they moved through the sprawling ranch house.

She thrust out her jaw. "No."

"Okay."

Erin kept going. They reached the game room and saw that the kids were just as her brother had described.

"Uh-oh," Sammy said.

Stevie, clearly punch-drunk with fatigue, giggled. "Busted!"

Heather laughed, too, apparently having too much fun to react to her father's frown.

"You all know better," Erin stated firmly.

"We couldn't help it. We weren't tired," Sammy said, already getting up to turn off the TV.

"You have school tomorrow," she reminded them.

"Daddy, can you lay down with me for a while, so I can go to sleep?" Heather asked.

"Yes, but that doesn't mean you're not in trouble," Mac said, taking her gently by the hand. "Because no matter what house we are in, the rules are still the rules."

He had a good point, Erin thought as she put her boys to bed. Rules were rules, and she hadn't been following any of her usual self-imposed restrictions since she'd met Mac.

If she kept acting so recklessly around him, she was going to have her heart broken all over again. And she really could not handle that.

MAC EMERGED from the bedroom, where his daughter was finally asleep, to find Gavin waiting for him in the living room downstairs. He gestured for Mac to join him.

"Maybe I didn't make myself clear earlier," Gavin said. "My sister has been through a lot."

"Losing her daughter."

"And having to put up with her louse of an ex-husband."

Ah, G.W. "None of you seem to like him, except for the boys."

Gavin scowled. "The boys seem to have largely forgotten—which is probably a good thing for them—but G.W. treated them all really badly when their baby sister was sick."

Mac tensed. "What do you mean?"

"I don't want to get into the details. That's for Erin to tell you—or not." Her brother's jaw set. "The point is, she's vulnerable. So are the kids. To have them all depend on having you and Heather around, or think this is going to lead to long-term happiness, is a mistake."

Was it? Mac wondered. Given email, videoconferencing and social media, it was easy to keep up with friends—no matter where they were. Plus he had the financial means to return to Texas for visits.

A long-term relationship was possible. If it was what everyone wanted. And he was beginning to think, given the intense way Erin had just been kissing him, that it was. "So what is it you would have me do?"

"Stop pursuing her romantically. My sister doesn't need to have her hopes raised, only to be left again."

"Gavin!" Erin interrupted, storming into the room. "None of this is for you to decide."

"I won't apologize for looking out for you," he grumbled.

"I'm a grown woman!"

"With a heart that's way too big."

Erin rolled her eyes. "You guys are all the same. You

worry too much. Seriously, bro, *I can handle this.*" She turned toward Mac. "A word? Outside?"

Erin switched on the lights in the yard and led the way out the back door. She looked so grim and determined, Mac couldn't help but joke, "Taking me to the woodshed?"

She tossed an indignant look over her slender shoulder. "To check on the horses. Given the fact you're working on your cowboy credentials and all."

The ranch horses had been turned out to pasture with plenty of water when they'd arrived home from their ride. Feed had been put out an hour after that, and now the half-dozen beauties were grazing sedately in the pasture next to the barn. Mac walked through the yellow glow of the outdoor lighting into the softer moonlight. "You going to bring them in for the night?"

Erin rested her arms on the pasture fence. "Not when it's so warm. I'll leave the barn doors open. Any horses who want shelter can have it. But most of the time they like to stay outside and enjoy the cool breeze at night—and maybe go inside in the shade if it gets too hot during the day."

"You've got it all worked out."

Her lip curved ruefully. "Horses are easy. Families are hard."

"Talking about Gavin?"

Finally, Erin turned to face Mac. "He means well."

"I know." Mac rested a forearm on the wooden fence and faced her, too. "I didn't take offense."

Erin searched his eyes. "What did he tell you?"

Mac shrugged. "That G.W. treated you and the kids badly when Angelica was sick. None of your siblings have quite forgiven him."

Erin's laugh was bitter. "That's pretty clear."

"And yet you have?"

She gestured helplessly. "It's complicated."

Mac moved closer, fighting the urge to take her in his arms. "Do you want to talk about it?"

She shook her head, looked away. He could feel her shutting down emotionally. "No," she said finally, looking out across the pasture again. "I want to talk about us. About what is going to happen when I don't sell the ranch to North Wind Energy."

This was news. "Have you decided that?"

"No. But I haven't decided I will, either. So…back to my question. If I say no?"

"I'll respect it." Mac touched her hand so she would look him in the eye. "Seriously. I have several other properties I am also looking at, and have talked with the owners. Like you, they are undecided, but I think I can work it out somewhere in Laramie County. And now that some of the county commissioners are on board…"

"But if it doesn't work out? For whatever reason."

He shrugged. "Then I'm on to my next assignment."

Silence fell. "Which would be?"

"Philadelphia."

Erin's brows knitted together.

"I'm going to request a position where I don't have to travel as much."

"Is that possible?" she asked skeptically.

"For lower pay and less responsibility, sure."

There was another pause, this one longer. "You'd do that?"

Mac exhaled. "Heather needs me more than she needs a big house in an exclusive neighborhood—or a prestigious private school—so yeah, I'd do that. I'm *going* to do that. For me, family is first, Erin." And it would be from now on.

She smiled. "For me, too."

"I GOT YOUR EMAIL and I'm absolutely horrified by what happened to you Friday evening!" Louise Steyn said over the phone Monday morning.

Mac had been afraid his boss would overreact.

"No sale is worth the health and welfare of one of our employees," she fumed.

"There's not going to be anymore trouble, because Prairie Natural Gas knows if there is, they'll be fired immediately, and out of the running for any future business in terms of the expansion."

"What's this about oil on the Triple Canyon Ranch?"

Briefly, Mac explained G. W. Decker's pitch to his ex-wife and her siblings. "Since the Monroes still hold the mineral rights, there could be money for them that way, too."

"Enough to turn down our proposal?"

Mac sighed. "Initially they rejected the idea out of hand, largely because of what it would do to the land. Putting the wind farm on the property poses the same problems. It would destroy the tranquility they enjoy now."

"So find them a smaller ranch closer to town that's for sale."

"It's not that simple," he said.

"It should be."

Silence fell.

"Mac, are you sure you're all right?" Louise cleared her throat. "You sound like you're in over your head, and I never thought I'd see the day that happened."

Mac hadn't, either. He'd spent his entire life trying to pull himself out of the poverty and chaos of his childhood, and through hard work and determination, had largely succeeded. Mainly because he forced himself to have a laser focus on whatever professional goal he set.

Now, thanks to the kindness of Erin Monroe, and her friends and family—as well as the many residents of Laramie, Texas—his views were much less pragmatic.

He couldn't stop thinking about how much he and Heather liked being here, or how much they had all enjoyed their Sunday afternoon ride on the ten-thousand-acre ranch. Texas—which had initially felt so foreign and folksy to him—was now like home. Erin was a definite romantic possibility.

And that was a shock.

He hadn't expected to get involved with a woman again, not until his daughter was grown and living on her own, anyway.

"Do you still want us to send the technical team to survey the property and prepare the estimated cost for the county commissioners?"

"Absolutely," Mac said. The sooner the business was done, the sooner he'd be able to make sense of his personal life and figure out if this thing with Erin was just a fling or something much longer lasting.

MAC SPENT THE REST of the day meeting with county commissioners and public utility executives, before picking up Heather at her Montessori school. She chatted nonstop about her day as he drove her back to the ranch. "So I guess you like it here," he murmured as they reached the ranch house.

"Daddy, I love it so much I don't ever want to leave!" Heather waved exuberantly at Sammy and Stevie, who were already home. Grinning, she handed Mac her backpack and raced over to shoot hoops with the boys.

Relieved that his daughter had adjusted to life in Texas so readily, Mac went on inside. Bridget and Bess were in the kitchen, one making a green salad, the other preparing pasta. Nicholas was setting the table. Erin, who usually manned the stove, was nowhere in sight.

"Hey, Mac," Bess said. "Dinner in twenty."

"Sounds good. Is there anything I can do?"

Bridget grinned. "Well, yeah. The dishes!"

"No problem." Stunned at how lonely it felt to him without their sister around, Mac asked casually, "Is Erin in her studio?"

Nicholas and the twins exchanged looks. "She's not going to be here tonight."

Erin hadn't mentioned that to him. Then again, it wasn't as if they had to check in with each other or ask permission. Mac nodded and went to wash up.

The meal was delicious. Yet something seemed off. Sammy and Stevie were more rambunctious than usual, cracking jokes and making Heather giggle. Bess, Bridget and Nicholas seemed distracted, aloof, despite their polite demeanor.

Once dinner was over, the kids were sent upstairs to do their homework. It seemed unusually quiet as Mac helped the Monroes clear the table and store the extra food in the fridge.

Dishrag in hand, Nicholas stared out the kitchen window. "It's going to be dark soon." He frowned. "Maybe one of us should go and check on Erin."

Bess and Bridget looked pained.

"I never know what to say," Bess said.

Her twin nodded. "I always feel like I make it worse."

"Make what worse?" Mac asked.

"The grieving," Bess explained.

ERIN WAS SITTING cross-legged in the grass. The overhead lights had switched on and the sun had gone down half an hour ago, leaving the cemetery cloaked in the scent of flowers and freshly mowed grass. She knew she should go home. She wanted to. But something kept her sitting right where she was. Thinking. Feeling. Wishing her life had turned out differently.

She was jolted from her thoughts when a vehicle came through the heavy wrought-iron gates and glided along the lane to a spot twenty yards away.

The door opened…and Mac got out.

He looked as solemn as the occasion demanded.

The tears she'd been fruitlessly trying to summon up and shed abruptly broke free. Moisture flowed from her eyes, blinding her.

He walked to her side. Knelt down. Took both her gloved hands in his.

The tears rained down all the harder.

He settled beside her and gathered her into his arms. A sob broke out, then another, and another.

Erin cried in a way she had never been able to cry, soaking his shirt and letting go of so much. Until finally the torrent ended. And the embarrassment returned.

"I'm s-s-sorry," she whispered.

Mac stroked her hair. "Your little girl would want you to cry, Erin. She'd want you to get it all out."

More tears welled up. "I can't."

"You are."

She supposed she was.

Erin drew back, saw that his face was wet, too.

She traced his tears with her fingertips, marveling that someone so big and strong and manly could also be gentle and sensitive. Kind. "How did you know I was here?"

He stroked a hand over her hair, cuddling her close. "Your siblings told me."

She leaned against his chest, listening to the strong beat of his heart. Briefly closing her eyes, she choked out, "Did they also tell you I'd be a mess?"

Mac kissed the top of her head, wrapped both arms around her and held on tight. "They said the second anniversary of Angelica's passing is coming up. You wanted to get the grave site ready, so it would be nice when you brought Sammy and Stevie over to see it."

"Not that it doesn't always look nice." Erin let out a shaky breath. "It does. But usually, there are silk flowers instead of pots of real ones. I tried keeping flowers going constantly the first year, because Angelica loved to plant flowers with me every spring. But the weather refused to cooperate…so I turned to silk ones during the times I knew it would be too hot or too cold, and containers of real ones the rest of the time."

He turned her face up to his, wiping away the tears that remained. "It looks nice."

Erin nodded, savoring his nearness and the comfort he offered. She dropped her head again. "I got them at Suzy Carrigan's greenhouse."

Silence fell between them. Lingered. Erin knew she should pull away, but stayed right where she was because it felt so right, sitting here, cuddled against him, with her head resting on his shoulder and his face pressed against her cheek.

Eventually, the need to keep talking—keep letting her feelings pour out—broke through. "I thought the first year would be the toughest."

Mac held her closer. "But it's not," he agreed. "The second one is worse, even though more time has elapsed, because the magical thinking has stopped."

Erin nodded miserably. "The finality of the death sinks in."

He stroked a hand down her spine. "The thought that you'll one day be together again in heaven seems like such small comfort."

She sighed. "When you want to be with your loved one so much right now." What she wouldn't give to be able to hold Angelica in her arms once more. She wondered if Mac felt the same way about his late wife.

"Your boys seem to be coping pretty well."

Erin nodded again. "It's been such a good distraction, having you and Heather here. It fills the void of losing their sister, and the divorce. Not that you're in any way acting like a husband."

Mac grinned.

"But they miss having a dad around, and you're a dad—and a good one—so it helps alleviate the pain."

Mac studied her. "Was G.W. a good dad? When he was around?"

She straightened away from him. "The kids love him. But deep down, they're angry with him, too. They know he should have been around a lot more when Angelica was sick, instead of hiding in his work." She released a quivering breath. "The chance to spend time with our daughter, to see her through those final, heart-wrenching days, was so precious. And so limited. He missed most of those last months with her, and I think he feels terrible guilt about it—and that, more than anything, is why he asked me for a divorce."

A tortured silence fell. "I'm not sure I could be so pragmatic or accepting, in your place," Mac said quietly.

Erin knew she was no saint. "It's not like I had any choice, Mac. He was leaving whether I wanted him to go or not."

"Did you ever ask him to stay?"

"Yes. Many times." To the point she knew she would never again beg a man to stay with her. "Don't get me wrong," she continued with a sigh. "I think our split was for the best. G.W. and I couldn't have stayed married and been happy. But I wish the kids had a complete family unit."

Mac nodded. "I wish the same thing. And I know that's the main reason Heather was so miserable before we got here, aside from disliking our new child-care arrangements and not getting along with the nanny I hired. She had that sense of belonging, with our family friends, whenever I had to work late or traveled. But all that changed when Joel, Anna and Stella moved away, when it was just the two of us. For the first time since we lost Cassandra, there was no surrogate mom, no sense of extended family...."

"She knew what she was missing," Erin offered.

"And she wanted a renewed sense of security. To the point..."

"What?"

Mac's expression turned rueful. "I don't think it will be all that long before Heather is asking me to get married again, so she can have a mom."

As Erin studied Mac, the intimacy between them deepened. And with it the sense that he had his own private burdens. "What about you?" she asked curiously. "Do you miss being married?"

Sensing she'd hit a nerve, she murmured, "Or was your marriage not all you wished it had been, either?"

Chapter Nine

Erin knew she shouldn't have asked. After all, it was none of her business. "Forget I said that." She gathered up her gardening tools and gloves. "Just because I'm spilling my guts here doesn't mean you have to spill yours."

"Maybe not, but—" Mac offered his hand and helped her to her feet. "Maybe I should."

Though he released his hold on her, the intimacy between them deepened.

"I don't think we ever would have gotten divorced. I think—because neither of us had any other living relatives—that we would have stayed married. But I don't think we would have ever been as happy as we could have been."

Erin picked up the empty flowerpots, while Mac retrieved the plastic water jugs. "Why not?" she asked as they wound their way through the cemetery to her car.

"Cassandra's childhood was as chaotic as mine was destitute," Mac confided. "As a consequence, when she grew up, she craved control of every aspect of her life. She couldn't compromise about anything."

Erin's heart went out to him.

"She wanted to stay in Philadelphia, where our friends were, even when my job required that I travel all over the Southwest."

"She refused to relocate?"

Mac nodded grimly. "And to get her occasional shortness of breath checked out."

"The pulmonary embolism."

He exhaled sharply. "I kept nagging her to see our family doc."

Had Cassandra done so, she might still be alive, Erin realized. They fell silent, thinking about that.

"But there were other things she wanted to control, too," Mac said eventually. "Like precisely when she got pregnant, where Heather was born, what she ate, wore, who her pediatrician was…those were all in Cassandra's domain. I had no say in any of it. Which isn't to say she made bad decisions. They were all fine."

"The point is, you were excluded."

He nodded. "And that wears on a person, too."

"You begin to resent them and then you feel bad for resenting them because they *are* doing a good job in regard to the family and finances and so on."

Mac slanted her a look as they neared Erin's SUV. "I thought marriage would be more of a partnership."

She smiled ruefully. "So did I."

Mac looked into her eyes. "Instead, it was almost like we were executives running two entirely different companies that only occasionally overlapped."

Erin set her things down on the ground and searched her pocket for her keys. "A lot of couples are happy living that way."

He shook his head. "I wasn't."

"Neither was I."

Their glances meshed again. "Who would have thought we would have that in common?" Erin asked wryly.

They exchanged brief smiles.

Getting back to business, she put all the gardening gear in the cargo area.

"So what now?" Mac asked, rocking back on his heels.

She turned to him. He looked so handsome in the moonlight, so kind. "I don't want to go home."

He rubbed a thumb over her cheek. "What would you like to do?"

Erin squinted. "Are you up for a little adventure?"

"With you?" His grin broadened. "Just show me when and where."

ERIN LOOK THE LEAD in her SUV and Mac followed close behind. Although he was prepared for just about anything, he was surprised to find them heading back to the ranch.

She'd said she hadn't wanted to go home.

But that was exactly where she took them. Or started to, anyway. They drove past the entrance to the Triple Canyon, past the thousand or so acres of fence line, to a barely noticeable gravel lane.

Erin turned onto it.

The road was so rough and bumpy it was tough going at fifteen miles an hour.

Their way lit by the swath of high-beam headlights, they continued deeper and deeper onto Monroe land. Up one hill, down another, across a flat plain, and then up a forty-five degree grade to what looked like a gravel parking area, next to several picnic tables beneath an open-air shelter.

Erin parked, cut the motor and got out.

Mac maneuvered his vehicle beside hers and did the same.

She walked around to the tailgate and handed him a small cooler. Then rummaged around until she found a battery-operated camping lantern that let out a soft yellow light. "Like a Girl Scout, you come prepared," Mac joked.

"Sort of. Right now, I'm wishing for a cold beer. All I've got is lemonade, an apple, a package of crackers and a hunk of cheese."

"Planning to picnic?" The ridge was windy and cool, and sported a view of the entire ranch, including the house and barns.

Erin shrugged. "I knew I wouldn't want to go home right away after being with Angelica. I always need time to decompress."

"And this is where you come?"

"For a couple of reasons. I have a lot of happy memories associated with this picnic area. My parents brought us here a lot when we were kids, and I continued the tradition with my own family. Angelica in particular loved it here."

"And..."

"It's also a place to rail against whatever you want to rail against."

He stared at her, fascinated by her in a way that continually surprised him. She was supposed to be a potential business quarry, yet was turning out to be so much more.

"I'm serious," Erin said recklessly as she edged closer. "You want me to demonstrate?"

Wanting her to get it all out, Mac nodded.

Erin walked toward the bluff. Standing about ten feet back, she looked up at the starlit sky, held her arms wide and let out a loud, long, relentlessly echoing shriek that seemed to come from her very soul.

Having released what was probably just the tip of her inner rage, she turned around and looked at him, almost daring him to expose even a fraction of those kind of raw emotions.

"Now you try it."

Mac shook his head. He wasn't the kind of guy to go around railing against the universe, even when his heart was broken. "Not really my thing."

She stepped closer, tilted her head up to his. "You don't have to yell in protest. You can yell like your team just won the Super Bowl."

That was maybe more his style. He grinned. "Is this a Monroe family tradition, too?"

Erin shoved her hands in the pockets of her jeans. "Nope…just mine."

Yet she was sharing it with him.

Asking him to join her.

He reached out to squeeze her shoulders, and stepped toward the ridge. "Better cover your ears."

Erin chuckled, moving with him. "You really think you can outyell me?"

"Are you kidding? I've got Philly blood."

He could tell by the way she was looking at him she didn't really think he was going to do it. So he lifted his arms, beat his chest and let out a battle cry that would have done any Texan proud.

By the time he'd finished, Erin was wincing. "Now let's do it together," she said.

They whooped and hollered until they had no more breath left. When Erin looked at him, he could tell she was still in pain. Truth was, she might never recover fully from such a devastating loss.

But there was still comfort to be had in this life. And he could tell by the way she was looking at him that she knew how to temporarily alleviate the pain as well as he did.

She moved closer.

He took her all the way into his arms.

Her face lifted. His lowered.

Her eyes drifted shut, and then her hands were in his hair and his mouth was on hers. Their lips were fused with a mixture of heat and compassion, understanding and tenderness.

Mac discovered he needed Erin as much as she needed him. Needed this. And he gave himself over to the experience completely, hauling her close so their bodies were touching in one long demanding line. Breasts to chest, stomach to stomach, thigh to thigh. Grasping her hips, he shifted her higher, until his hardness pressed against the apex of her thighs. With a low moan of surrender, she climbed his body and wrapped her legs around his waist.

Still kissing her, Mac carried her to the picnic area. Stepping into the gazebo, he sank down on a picnic table. The camping lantern, combined with the moonlight overhead, provided a soft romantic atmosphere that was perfect for lovemaking.

Erin straddled his lap. "Make me forget," she pleaded, unbuttoning her blouse with one hand. "Help me live."

And live they did, as Mac finished the job she'd started, in a moment that stretched toward the future. Their future. He opened her shirt and unhooked her bra, divesting her of both. "You're so beautiful," he whispered, knowing he'd never wanted a woman the way he wanted Erin. "So feminine and perfect."

"You make me feel perfect," she whispered back.

Her erect nipples pressed against his palms when he cupped her breasts, reveling in her voluptuousness...and her sweet womanly fragrance. Impatient, Erin unbuttoned his shirt and took it off in turn.

She smiled as she admired his broad shoulders and rippled chest. "I never knew a *man* could be so beautiful," she said, tracing his pecs with her fingertips.

Mac joked, "It's all in the eye of the beholder." And she was looking at him as if he was God's gift.

He kissed her deeply, testing the silky heat of her mouth and the soft give of her lips beneath his. She moaned in response. His body hardening, he delved even more erotically, stroking her tongue with his.

She kissed him back, surrendering completely. "Then we've both found the right beholders," she said when they finally came up for air.

"No kidding." Wanting to give her the release she so richly deserved—and needing room to maneuver—Mac shifted Erin off his lap. Naked from the waist up, he stood, offered her his hand. "If we're going to do this, I want you to be comfortable."

Hand in hand, they moved toward his SUV. He opened up the rear, reached in to fold the middle seat down, then turned back to her. She was gorgeous. Ready. Waiting. Feeling his own body go up in flames, he unbuckled and unzipped. Erin followed suit. Naked, they stretched out inside the vehicle and lay on their sides, facing each other. Mac nuzzled her throat, her collarbone, then kissed her as if they had all the time in the world. As if this moment in time, the way they were, was all that mattered.

With every minute that passed, Erin lost herself more in his tender caresses. "Mac…" she whispered, undulating against him.

"Not yet." She wasn't ready. Making his way to her breasts, he paid homage to her nipples.

"I…"

Deliberately, he shifted her onto her back. "We're not rushing this. Close your eyes." Lowering his head, he put his mouth on her, using his lips and tongue, making her arch up and start to come.

But that wasn't good enough. Grasping her ankles, he

shifted her legs upward, until her knees were bent, her feet flat on the carpet. He trailed kisses over her abdomen, went lower still. "Open yourself up for me."

He was asking the impossible, Erin knew.

It wasn't going to happen.

Much as she wanted and needed release, there was a part of her—a strong part—that was still numb, still heartbroken, still resisting. A part of her that refused to lose herself in passion or the wonderful man beside her. A part of her that said the one night of pleasure they'd already had was enough. It was all she was going to get.

But of course, Mac didn't agree.

He knew she could—and had—climaxed with earth-shattering intensity. And he was determined it would happen again. Even if it meant stopping and taking stock of the situation, sliding upward and kissing her again. Not as a prelude to what followed, but as a pleasure all on its own. As if kissing was an orgasmic act in itself, something to lose yourself in. And she did.

The next thing Erin knew, her knees were falling open of their own volition, and he was between her spread thighs. Pulling her toward the edge of the vehicle, Mac lowered his lips once again.

Skin touched skin and the world skittered to a stop.

All Erin knew was the erotic intensity of his mouth and the tender stroking of his hands. And right now, as he explored every inch of her feminine core, she was all woman, she was vulnerable, she was all his. He held her until she stopped shuddering, then moved upward.

"My turn." Hand to his shoulder, she shifted him onto his back.

Muscles taut, he looked lovingly into her eyes. "Sure you want to wait?" he murmured. "You're ready now."

"Ready for you," she stipulated. "Ready for this."

He groaned as her silky hair slid across his abdomen. She licked her way down his ribs, let her hair fall lower still. "And you're ready for me, too. Well," she said playfully, eager to meet his desires as thoroughly as he had hers, "maybe not *quite.*"

"Erin..."

Savoring the heat and hardness of his body, she gripped his thighs. "Let me do this, Mac. Let me adore you."

And she did. When he could stand it no more, he took her by the waist and lifted her upward. Curved over his body, her hands on his shoulders, she straddled his lower abdomen and rose on her knees. "Now?" she whispered, lowering herself slowly.

He moaned at the feel of their bodies joining. "Now."

She tightened around him as they became one. He surged and withdrew, and surged again. Until there was nothing but this moment in time, and the feel of each other. Nothing but this passion and the inevitable explosion of feeling and need. Erin soared and Mac followed close behind. Together, they found everything they had ever wanted, and everything they had ever needed.

ERIN COLLAPSED ON Mac's chest, tingling and shuddering all over, still breathing hard. To her relief, the emotional numbness that seemed so much a part of her was gone. In its place was a disquieting mixture of elation and regret.

She had sworn she wouldn't do this again. Add more confusion to an already difficult situation.

Yet when she was alone with Mac, all she could think about was putting aside all the problems, all her heartache, and being with him like this. It was crazy. It was risky. And real.

"I'm not sure what was more effective, this or the

primal screams," Mac whispered against her neck. "All I know is that I haven't felt this free in a long time."

Erin snuggled close. "I know what you mean. I come up here every now and again to let out my rage against the unfairness of life. But usually all I feel afterward is hoarse and limp with exhaustion."

His lips curved against her skin. "And now?"

"I'm hoarse and limp with satisfaction."

He ran a hand down her spine.

Erin rose slightly, resting her head on her palm. "Do you ever feel guilty about going on?"

Swallowing hard, he nodded.

She sighed. "Me, too."

Mac smoothed her hair. "I think about all the what-ifs. What if I had convinced Cassandra to go to the doctor sooner? Would they have found the embolism? Been able to save her?"

Erin understood. "What if I had seen some sign of Angelica's cancer a lot sooner? Would they have been able to arrest the tumor? Would she still be alive today?"

Silence reigned.

"But it always comes back to the same thing." Erin rolled onto her back and dropped her forearm over her eyes. "Life is what it is. I think we're all on these paths that are somehow predestined or heaven-made—and with the exception of little variations, we're all going to end up wherever we were destined to."

Mac shifted onto his side to study her. "It stinks, not being able to control everything in our lives, doesn't it?"

"It does." She reached for his hand. "But what's great are moments like this," she confessed, entwining her fingers with his. "Moments that are quite extraordinary. Moments that seem, in their own way, predestined, too."

Mac thought about that. "You think we were meant to meet?" he murmured, kissing her knuckles.

"And be the catalyst each other needs? Yes. I do." Erin held his eyes a long moment.

"Maybe we should just accept this for the gift that it is, a way to get to the next stage of recovery of our losses."

"And not worry beyond that," Erin agreed.

Mac shrugged. "Makes sense, don't you think? Given all we've got on our agendas..."

He was right about that, Erin conceded, as she reluctantly pushed her more romantic notions aside.

He had a business deal to complete, with or without her and Monroe land. He had Heather to care for, and a new nanny to find...back in Philadelphia.

Erin had to make a decision about the Triple Canyon Ranch's future, honor the anniversary of her daughter's passing...and somehow get through the upcoming Mother's Day holiday. Not to mention keep her relationship with Mac in the "satisfying fling" category.

Maybe it was best not to think too much.

She slid back into Mac's arms. "I agree. The smartest thing to do right now is take it one day, one moment, at a time." And she knew, as their lips fused together once again, right where she wanted this particular moment to lead.

MAC AND ERIN STAYED on the bluffs for most of the night, making love and talking, eventually tiptoeing back to the house around 4:00 a.m.

Their time together had been really cathartic. Erin felt as if a huge burden of grief and guilt and misery had been exorcised from her body.

When morning came, way too soon, the sun was shining. It looked like the beginning of a beautiful May day.

"You'll never guess what happened last night, while you and Mac were gone," Sammy said. "Dad called!"

Erin was surprised; that happened only once in a blue moon. "Really?"

"And guess what else!" Stevie reported. "He told us he's coming to see us on field day at school, this Thursday. He said he wants to see us compete!"

"Isn't that great?" Sammy beamed, adding more cereal and milk to his bowl.

It certainly would be, Erin thought, if G.W. showed up. Determined not to be the Debbie Downer of the situation, she flashed a bright smile. "I'm excited, too."

"We're going to really have to practice our running and jumping after school today," Sammy told Stevie, who was having seconds, too. "'Cause I want Dad to see me win!"

"Me, too!"

The boys were still chattering away when Heather came down to the breakfast table.

Erin looked at the child's sullen, bereft expression and became immediately concerned, as did her sons. "Is everything okay?" Erin asked Mac, who arrived right after her.

"Heather says she doesn't feel well," he said. He put a hand to his daughter's forehead, then frowned. "But I don't think she's running fever."

Erin knelt in front of her. "Can you tell us what's wrong?"

Heather averted her eyes and gave a slight shrug.

Was it possible the little girl sensed that something had shifted between the two of them? Erin wondered. Even if only temporarily?

Oblivious to the drama, Bess and Bridget came into the kitchen, backpacks in tow. The twins had offered to drop Sammy and Stevie at school en route to the university.

"What's going on?" Bess asked. She was dressed in the scrubs she wore to her nursing laboratory courses.

"Heather's feeling a little out of sorts," Erin explained. "You-all can go on."

Sammy and Stevie both stiffened. The escalating worry on their faces made Erin realize they must be recalling a time when another "little sister" hadn't felt so well. "It's okay," she assured them with an "everything's under control" smile. "Mac and I will handle it. And I'll see you guys at the store after school."

They relaxed only slightly.

The twins realized what was going on. They commiserated with Heather and then hustled the boys out the door. Gavin and Nicholas had already gone, so Mac and Erin were left with his daughter.

"Did something happen at school?" Mac asked.

Heather blinked. They were getting close, Erin thought.

"Did you have a fight with another student? Get in trouble with the teacher?"

Again, there was no response.

Erin looked at Mac. "Was there anything in her backpack? A note, maybe?"

"Good idea." He opened up Heather's bag and pulled out a pink mimeographed sheet. Reading it, he sighed heavily, then handed it to Erin.

She skimmed it. No wonder the little girl was upset. Sensing Mac was at a loss how to handle it, Erin knelt down near Heather. "Is this about the Mother's Day tea on Friday?" she asked gently, when they were at eye level.

Tears welled. Head downcast, Heather rubbed the toe of her new cowgirl boot across the floor. "W-we have to make a special present for our mommies and I don't have a mommy anymore." Her small shoulders slumped.

"So," she concluded in a voice thick with tears, "I don't want to go."

Why did schools do things like this? Erin wondered, incensed, knowing it likely wasn't just Mac's child being affected here. Couldn't teachers figure out how to celebrate events in a way that wouldn't leave less fortunate children feeling more excluded and heartbroken than they already were?

Mac looked helplessly at Erin. "This is the kind of thing that Joel and Anna would have stepped in to help with."

"But Miss Anna isn't here anymore," Heather sobbed. "And now I don't have anybody to go with me!"

Mac knelt and scooped his daughter into his arms. "Honey, you don't have to go alone," he promised, rubbing her back. "I'll go with you. You can make whatever it is you're making at school for me instead."

"But you're not a mommy!" Heather said brokenly, thrusting out her lower lip.

And anything other than a "mommy" or appropriate female substitute in this situation wouldn't do. Impulsively, Erin looked the little girl in the eye and offered, "I am, though. And if you'd like, I'd be honored to take you to the tea."

Chapter Ten

"Are you sure you're up to this?" Darcy Purcell asked Erin later that morning. "A Mother's Day tea?"

"It'll be fine."

"Are you sure?" her best friend pressed.

Actually, no, Erin thought. She wasn't. She'd done nothing but fret over how she was going to be able to handle all the moms and their precious little daughters since she'd made the impulsive decision.

Would going to the event break her heart all the more, by reminding her of all she had lost when she'd buried her daughter? Or would it be a bittersweet event, bringing back memories of Angelica in a way that comforted her? Most important, would she be able to stay as present for Heather, and give the still-grieving child what she needed?

Not about to admit that, after already promising the distraught little girl she'd go, Erin went back to working on Mac's boots. "I need to do a good deed every now and then." Carefully, she glued the inside linings to the outer leather pieces. "Otherwise how am I going to get to heaven?"

Darcy rolled her eyes at the joke and continued wrapping up a pair of boots for another customer. "Are you kidding me? You're definitely going to heaven! And as for good deeds, you do plenty of those. The most talked about at the moment is the way you've taken in Mac and his little girl."

Erin stitched two glued pieces of leather together. "After the way he got roughed up, it was the neighborly thing to do."

"The way you talk about them, it seems like it's more than that. Like maybe they're filling a hole in your life. Since..." *Angelica died.*

Guilt flooded Erin, that anything or anyone could ease her grief. The loss of her daughter was a pain that would never go away.

No matter how much she tried to move on, it was still there every day, like a knife in her heart.

Darcy hugged her. "I'm sorry, Erin. I didn't mean to upset you. I know what a tough time of year this is for you."

"You're not upsetting me. I'm already upset." And yet, with Mac and Heather in her life, the pain was a lot more bearable.

Was it possible the two of them were heaven sent?

That, as she and Mac had supposed, they had crossed paths for a reason? Because she could help him and his little girl, and he could help her deal with the loss of her daughter?

The bell rang, signaling the first customers of the day. Darcy disappeared. Erin heard voices downstairs, but kept right on working. Footsteps sounded on the stairs.

Darcy was back, with their local postal worker and the PTA president from Laramie Elementary School behind her.

Zelda Arnett handed over the day's stack of mail to Erin, then lingered a moment, as she often had since

Angelica had died, to chat a little and make sure Erin was doing okay.

Beside her, the copper-haired PTA president was on a mission. Marybeth Simmons tore off a sheet from the clipboard in her hand. "Hey, Erin," she said crisply. "I'm here to remind you about the field day. You're signed up to time the fifty-yard dash for the fifth graders, and we'll probably draft you to help with other events as needed."

Erin scanned the details regarding participation, then smiled and tacked the sheet on the bulletin board above her worktable. "No problem," she said cheerfully. "I'll be there."

"With your sunscreen on and an ice pack handy," Zelda teased with a warning lift of a silver eyebrow beneath the wide-brimmed hat she wore with her uniform. "Thursday is going to be a scorcher."

They groaned in unison.

It seemed as if spring had leaped into summer, with few really nice days in between. Where was all that balmy eighty-degree weather they had longed for all winter? Instead, it was in the mid-nineties nearly every day.

"I see you got your electric bill, too." Marybeth frowned. "Don't faint when you read it."

Curious, Erin opened the envelope. Sighing, she wondered what it would cost to keep the store comfortably cool when summer came around and temperatures climbed past a hundred every single day.

"And don't forget to take a look at the notice the public utility tucked in there," Marybeth advised, frowning all the more. "There's going to be a rate hike starting in June, which they hope to do away with once a decision is made on how to expand."

"Well, it can't come soon enough," Zelda said. "And I have to tell you, Erin, I think it's wonderful what you and your family are doing, sacrificing your ranch land for this new wind farm."

Startled, Erin held up a cautioning hand. "That hasn't been decided."

Marybeth's eyes widened. "Everyone says it has. That Mac Wheeler couldn't be more confident."

Talk about the caboose getting ahead of the train! "Mr. Wheeler knows we're still thinking about it," Erin stated firmly.

The PTA president dug in her heels. "But the decision about what to do with Monroe land is really yours, isn't it? I mean, isn't that the way it's always been?"

It *was,* Erin thought, as the bell rang again and more footsteps sounded on the stairs. Mac Wheeler strode into the workshop as if he owned the place.

Zelda batted her eyelashes and laid a hand over her heart. "Well, speak of the devil."

"WHAT WAS THAT ALL ABOUT?" Mac asked when the three women had scattered, leaving Erin to speak with him in private.

"The word around these parts is that the wind farm on Monroe land is already a done deal. You wouldn't know where that talk is coming from, would you?" Erin said, as she attached two pieces to the top of the boot and sewed them together.

Mac's expression was all-innocence as he set down his briefcase. "Not me. I don't count my chickens before they hatch."

"You said something earlier about looking at other land. Is that still a possibility?"

He nodded. "I've found two more ranches perfectly suited to hold some or all of the three hundred forty-two

of the mold while they dried. Finished, she took off her work apron and hung it on the hook by the door. "I kind of think I do, since you paid triple to get them in time for the meeting with the county commissioners next week."

"That was before I demonstrated my ability to feint and duck and stay light on my feet. And deliver a mean right hook."

Erin glanced at him wryly. "As long as you're modest."

"Very much so."

Overhead, the lights of her studio flickered.

"Oh, no," she said as the power cut out completely and everything went dark.

"Talk about perfect timing." Mac found her in the utter blackness. He pulled her against him.

Despite her earlier decision to remain immune—at least until she'd made a decision about the land—Erin sank into his body heat. He smelled every bit as good as he felt. "You think someone's trying to tell me something?"

He leaned in close and his breath brushed her earlobe. "Up above, or at the county electric plant?"

A thrill swept through her at his nearness. "Ha, ha."

"I think this blackout is random." He kissed her temple, then her cheek. "But in my favor nevertheless."

Erin sighed, her longing to be loved getting the better of her judgment. "How do you figure that?"

Mac sifted his hands through her hair and kissed her other temple. "Because I've missed you. And I've been thinking about you. And now have the chance to show you."

He pulled her full against him. Common sense warred with her desire. Erin splayed her hands across his chest. "Mac. We can't. Not here… Not now…" Not when Nicholas and the twins and Gavin were all still awake…

"I know." Mac tenderly kissed her lips. "The flashlight brigade will be here any second to rescue us."

Erin shook her head. "They all know I have a lantern out here."

Chuckling, Mac kissed her even more deeply. "Then do us both a favor and don't find it just yet."

Erin groaned and held on to the only solid thing she could reach—him. Which led to another kiss, and another. Who knew what would have happened next had the lights not suddenly come back on? She blinked in surprise, stumbled backward.

Mac stared at her, still wanting her.

She stared at him as the seconds ticked out.

And just when she thought she couldn't handle another decision, never mind another surprise, a host of cars sounded in the driveway and a delegation of ranchers arrived.

Suffice it to say, they weren't happy.

AT ERIN'S SUGGESTION, Mac ushered the boisterous group into the living room. He heard the cowboys out for the better part of an hour. The chief complaint, Erin noted, was the way the big structures would disfigure the ruggedly gorgeous terrain. "That many turbines will be a blight on the countryside," cattle rancher Emmett Briscoe fumed.

Mac leaned forward, hands clasped between his knees. "That's why we're proposing to locate them all in one area," he explained.

"You'll ruin this ranch if you put them here. It'll be more of an outdoor factory than a picturesque haven." Amy Carrigan-McCabe, who grew landscape plants on her property, was all about natural beauty.

"What happens to the turbines when the wind dies

down?" horse rancher Kelsey Lockhart-Anderson asked. "There are days when there is zero wind velocity."

"And others," Mac countered pleasantly, "where it's storm force. Luckily, the wind turbines are built to handle all wind speeds, and excess electricity can be stored for future use."

Reba Cartwright asked, "What about the noise?"

"There will be some," Mac admitted. "But the turbines are going to be a hundred feet in the air, so much of the sound will dissipate above us."

"Look," Mac continued affably. "When I first came here, I admit I didn't get it. I was proposing cheap, affordable, clean energy—and plenty of it—and I expected the citizens of Laramie County to jump at the opportunity to be part of the wave of future."

But they hadn't been, Erin knew.

"Then events beyond my control had me accepting Erin's hospitality and actually living on a ranch temporarily, and I began to see the individual character of each of these ranches and the powerful sense of family that comes from each ranch, where generation upon generation built these homesteads into what they are. So I appreciate all of you wanting to keep everything exactly as is." Mac paused. "But I've also been around for some of the rolling blackouts, and we all know those are going to get worse, especially in the rural areas, because that's where the utility company can cut power sporadically and affect the fewest number of residents."

Members of the group began to look troubled.

Mac continued soberly, "There are other ways to remedy that particular problem, of course. You could all invest in generators, but those are expensive, too, and most of the ones built nowadays for personal use don't power very much for very long." He shrugged. "I mean, they'll run your fridge, freezer or air-conditioning unit, but not a lot else, and usually not everything at the same time."

"I've priced 'em," Brady Anderson said. "Units are running nearly ten thousand dollars to install, for very little return in the way of actual power produced. And whatever generator you put in has to run on some sort of fuel, so you're looking at installing a big oil or propane tank on your property, since most of us this far out don't have natural gas provided to our homes."

"That's true," Erin murmured. "We have a wood-burning stove for emergencies, but everything else here is run by electricity, via the overhead power lines. Which, when you think about it, aren't all that attractive, either. They're just an accepted part of the landscape."

Mac nodded, clearly appreciating her support. "The solution to the escalating shortage lies in substantially adding to the power grid for the entire county. So that as you improve your ranches—and take a lot of your agricultural operations into the future—you'll be able to fuel them. Or maybe, if you aren't interested in that, you'll simply be able to save money, with lower power bills."

Rebecca Carrigan-McCabe, an alpaca rancher, observed, "But what's the reality of having something this big and noisy in our backyard? What's it going to do to our herds?"

Hers was a valid concern, Erin knew. Alpacas were easily spooked. Would the sound of the turbines carry as far as the Primrose Ranch, a few miles down the highway?

Mac responded practically. "Experience has shown us that the animals will get used to it as quickly as we humans do. But seeing is believing. Which is why I'd like to put together a bus tour of two other North Wind Energy projects in the Panhandle. It'll be a day trip. Completely free of charge to anyone who wants to go." Talk continued a little while longer. Nearly everyone in the room promised to go on the bus tour to get a better idea of what they'd be facing. Finally, all the ranchers left. Only Mac and Erin, and Nicholas, who had sat in on the impromptu meeting, remained.

"I've never seen anyone calm a crowd so fast," Nicholas murmured. "How did you learn to do that?"

Mac helped Erin collect the coffee mugs. "Years of training and experience. When you're trying to sell to someone, the first thing you have to do is understand whatever negative emotions they are having. That tells you what the obstacles are."

Nicholas looked thoughtful. "Like if a person is trying to buy a car, but is worried it will cost too much."

Mac nodded. "But let's say they really want a new vehicle, and not just any car, but a Ford Mustang convertible circa 1964. You know it's out of their price range. They know it's out of their price range."

"But they still really want it."

"You'll get a sale if you can find something they can afford that has all the attributes of the vehicle they want."

"So in this case," Nicholas mused, "with the wind farm..."

"People are afraid of what they don't know, and worry that it's going to infringe on their lives in ways they don't like," Mac said.

"So what do you do?" Nicholas asked.

He spread his hands. "Find a place where it will do the least damage."

"Like our ranch," the youth concluded.

Mac cast a sideways look at Erin and cleared his throat. "I've looked into other locations, but so far none of the owners are interested...."

Nicholas's brow furrowed. "So right now, the Triple Canyon Ranch is the only viable option?"

"It's the starting place," Mac affirmed with another consoling look at Erin. "However, it may not be the ending place."

But it was where everyone, including the neighboring ranchers, expected the wind farm to be placed.

Awhirl with emotion, Erin ducked into the mudroom, and from there slipped out into the backyard. Mac and Nicholas were still talking intently inside, but out here, the night was beautiful. A quarter moon shone and a symphony of stars dotted the wide velvet sky.

Erin walked across the yard, past the barn, to the fence.

The horses were scattered across the pasture, grazing sedately. What would happen to them if she sold? Erin wondered, inhaling the fresh scents of green grass and flowers. Would she be able to find a place so perfect? Would she and the boys have somewhere to ride?

She drew a shaky breath. And what about the family? If she moved—because frankly, she couldn't see herself living in a house surrounded by 342 hundred-foot-high turbines—would her siblings immediately get places of their own?

Deep down, she feared it wouldn't be just the legacy of their ancestors that they would be losing, but they could also be jeopardizing the close, intimate bond between the current generation of Monroes.

"I thought I might find you out here."

Erin turned to see Mac approaching. He looked even sexier in the moonlight. "Did Nicholas go on to bed?" she asked.

Mac joined her at the pasture fence. "To his room. He said he has a little homework to finish before he turns in." Their gazes collided. "Thanks for hosting that impromptu meeting tonight," Mac said eventually.

Telling herself she was not going to end up kissing him again, Erin looked away. "Meeting or lynching?"

Mac's smile was contagious. "It certainly started out the latter."

Her own smile fading, Erin sighed and looked out at the horses again. "Until your legendary charm and salesmanship turned it around, anyway."

Mac edged close enough for her to feel his body heat. He turned so his back was to the fence, his face to hers. "Are you upset because I'm good at what I do, or because I taught Nicholas some of the tricks of the trade?"

How about I'm upset because you seem to have succeeded? And I don't know where any of it leaves me. Knowing that would sound selfish, Erin shook off her melancholy. "Pay no attention. I'm just in a terrible mood."

He studied her, taking in her cool attitude. "Because?"

"Countless reasons. The anniversary of Angelica's passing. Mother's Day." *The prospect of you and Heather leaving Texas to go back to Philly...* She'd come to count on having them under her roof, seeing them at mealtimes, and so much more....

Misunderstanding, Mac offered, "If you'd like to back out of the tea—"

"No." Erin stopped him, a hand on his arm. "I'm going," she said firmly. It was the one thing she was sure about. "That event will be fine. Track-and-field day at Laramie Elementary School, on the other hand, may not be so great." Deciding they'd stood in the moonlight long enough, Erin turned and led the way back to the ranch house. "G.W. promised the boys he would show up."

The grass was damp from the dew and spongy beneath their feet. "And you're worried your ex-husband won't?"

Erin slid her hands in her pockets. "If he doesn't it won't be the first time."

"Hopefully, that won't be the case," Mac countered with a long, reassuring look. "But if it is, we'll deal with it."

"Together," Erin guessed.

"Yes."

Knowing how much her boys adored Mac, Erin liked the sound of that very much. Somehow, it helped knowing that if G.W. bailed on them again, this time she would have Mac by her side to weather the storm. It wasn't a forever kind of solution, since eventually he would head back to Philadelphia with Heather. But for now, for this moment, it was something.

Chapter Eleven

"It's so kind of you to offer to help today, Mr. Wheeler," the PTA president said when Mac walked into the Laramie Elementary School gymnasium at nine o'clock the next morning.

Erin, who was already there—passing out T-shirts and other field-day paraphernalia—waved at him from across the gym.

Mac smiled and waved back. "Erin told me about the email that went out last night, that if you didn't get more volunteers you were going to have to cancel some of the events. I didn't want the kids to be disappointed."

And he especially didn't want Sammy and Stevie, who'd been practicing their running and jumping all week, to feel let down. It was enough that their dad might not show up, after promising he would.

"Nor do we," Marybeth exclaimed. "Luckily, we were able to get five more volunteers at the last minute, so we'll be able to host all the events." She arched a brow. "Do you feel comfortable counting sit-ups?"

"Whatever you need," Mac said affably.

"Great! We're going to set up for that on the mats next to the rope climb. So if you want to head over to get your spirit shirt and gear, you'll be all set...."

Mac headed for Erin…and the sight of her took his breath away.

Her golden curls were swept into a ponytail. Her face held the glow of physical activity. She looked incredibly pretty in sneakers, khaki knee-length shorts and the bright green field-day T-shirt that everyone seemed to be wearing.

Her eyes held his as he neared, trying hard, it appeared, not to look as mesmerized as he felt.

"What do you think?" Darcy scanned Mac's shoulders, chest and abs with a critical eye, then turned to her. "Extra large? Or extra extra large?"

Erin's eyes roved his torso, reminding Mac of how she'd seemed to drink him in when they'd made love. His body tautened in response.

Her tongue snaked out to wet her lips. "I'm not sure. These are running a little small." She shrugged, eyeing Mac's chest again. "Maybe the larger one?"

Darcy handed him a folded shirt. "Let's have a look," she said.

Not sure what they expected him to do, he opened it up. Laramie Elementary School Annual Track and Field Day was emblazoned on the front. A large koala bear, the school mascot, decorated the back.

Darcy looked at Erin. "Help the man! Size him!"

Flushing slightly and refusing to look him in the eye, Erin stepped forward. She held up the XL size to Mac's chest. Pursed her lips thoughtfully, then stepped back. Still squinting at him, she reached for the XXL, held that up and let out a satisfied sigh. "Much better." She looked at Darcy. "Don't you think?"

Her best friend grinned, clearly in matchmaking mode. "I think you should be asking him," she teased, "while I go find out what we're going to be having for our picnic lunch." She sashayed off, still grinning.

"I haven't, but when—" *if* "—I do I'll tell him you're looking for him."

"Thanks, Mac." Stevie embraced Mac and resumed his place in line.

And so it went. Erin's boys spent the entire day scanning the crowds, looking for G.W. By the time the participation ribbons were passed out at two-thirty, both were visibly upset about his absence. Mac couldn't blame them.

"Anyone up for some ice cream?" he asked that evening, after a dinner of take-out pizza and salad.

Sammy shook his head and glanced down at the rainbow of blue, red and green ribbons pinned to his spirit shirt.

"Nah. No thanks, Mac," Stevie mumbled.

"They can't eat because they're sad, Daddy," Heather announced. "Because their daddy didn't show up today when he was s'posed to." She looked at the boys, clearly sharing their pain.

Her face tight with repressed anger, Erin got up to clear the table.

"Well, maybe it would help to ride your bikes a little before bath time." Sensing Erin needed some time alone to compose herself, Mac stood. "Come on, everyone. I'll go with you."

As they walked over to the garage, he asked casually, "So what are you guys going to do with your ribbons?"

They looked at each other, shrugged.

"I don't know," Stevie said.

"I was going to show my dad," Sammy reflected sadly.

"You still can. Next time you see him." Whenever that was.

"Nah," Sammy and Stevie said in tandem, with an acceptance that broke Mac's heart.

Sammy kicked at the ground. "He probably wouldn't care, anyway."

Maybe not. But they were just kids. And it wasn't the kind of situation they should be dealing with.

Mac gazed fondly at the boys. "Well, *I* care."

"So do I," Heather declared.

"And I know your mom is very proud of you," Mac continued, clapping a congratulatory hand on each boy's shoulder. "I mean, think about it. You got green ribbons for everything you participated in, red ribbons for every challenge you completed, and blue ribbons for every event where you scored in the highest range. You each came home with ten ribbons. That's pretty darn impressive if you ask me."

Slowly, the boys began to grin.

"You're really proud of us?" Sammy asked.

Mac felt emotion well in his chest. "I really am." He hugged each boy in turn, then turned to embrace his daughter, too. "And I'm really glad I got to come to your school today and be a part of it."

"Next time," Heather declared, "I want to go there, too."

"Go where?" Erin said, coming up behind them.

Mac could tell from the look on her face that she still seemed to be simmering with anger. "Track and field day at Laramie Elementary," he explained.

"No, Daddy," Heather corrected, "I want to *live here*. And go to Laramie Elementary School with Sammy and Stevie—not just for one day, but all the time."

"YOUR LITTLE GIRL REALLY knows what she wants," Erin told Mac an hour and a half later. Heather hadn't stopped talking about Texas and public school, and was still going on about it as Erin and Mac tucked all the kids into bed.

"That she does," Mac joked as the two of them walked out onto the back porch to enjoy what was left of the sunset.

Erin sank down on the cushioned swing. "Seriously, thanks for saying whatever it was you said to the boys after dinner. They seemed a lot better."

Mac settled beside her, so close their hips and shoulders touched. "I just told them how proud I was of them, what a good job they did."

Erin passed on the opportunity to move farther away. "I'm glad you were able to see it."

His hand covered hers. "Me, too."

A comfortable silence fell as they swung gently back and forth. "Speaking of feeling better, you seem a little less upset," he noted at last.

There was, Erin knew, a reason for that. "I called G.W. He didn't answer, but I left a message on his voice mail, telling him exactly what I thought of his actions." She sighed. "He probably won't be too happy with me. But this once, his absence was so hurtful to the kids, I felt I had to do it."

Mac slanted her a glance. "Do you think he'll get the message?"

"I wish he would, but…he probably won't. When he does show up he'll be full of excuses, saying he tried his hardest to be here for them, but work got in the way, yada yada yada."

Mac tightened his hand around hers. "How will the boys react if and when that happens?"

Erin closed her eyes. "I'm sure they'll forgive him, because G.W. will try to buy them off with an elaborate gift of some sort. Whatever it is, it will be over the top, he'll be all smiles, and their hearts will be mended once again." Erin shifted so she could look at Mac's face. "But

I don't want to talk about my ex-husband. I want to talk about you and your heroics today. You surprised everyone, Mac, by showing up at field day."

"Even me."

Perplexed, she wrinkled her brow.

"It's not the kind of thing I usually do."

She could believe that. The man who'd come to Texas a few weeks ago was a business-suit-and-briefcase kind of guy. Slowly, inevitably, as he'd continued to hang out in their casual, close-knit community, all that had changed.

Determined to be honest, she let him know about the gossip currently making the rounds. "Half the people think you volunteered today to further establish yourself as a good guy and up your popularity with the residents. They figure that if the ranch folks of Laramie are more inclined to support the wind farm, then your proposal will be a shoo-in with the county. After all, the commissioners always vote the way the majority of the constituents want."

"And the other half?"

"Think you were doing it to score points with me."

Erin couldn't believe she had blurted that out. Since she had, she watched for his reaction.

His face remained maddeningly implacable.

Mac searched her eyes. "And what do you think?"

Erin thought about it, then said, "I think you did it for the kids."

"Hmm."

"So which is it?" she insisted playfully, when he offered nothing more.

He shrugged and continued holding her hand. "Would you believe all three?"

"You're going to have to explain that one."

His smile widened. "I am a good guy. I don't mind people knowing that. Volunteering today gave me a chance to get to know a lot of the other parents in the community better."

Erin inhaled the clean, just-showered scent of him. "And you needed to do that because..."

He looked at her a long moment. "I'm thinking maybe Heather needs something other than city life. Maybe it's time I sold our apartment in the city and started looking for a small, suburban town for us to live in. I think she—we—might be happier."

"And the other reasons?" Erin probed, aware how right it felt, sitting with him like this, after the kids were all in bed.

Mac sobered. "I wanted Sammy and Stevie to feel supported. If their dad wasn't going to be there—and your brothers, who usually stand in for him in some way, couldn't, either—I wanted to be there for the boys."

Gratitude mixed with something stronger. "And you were," Erin stated with heartfelt sincerity. "And you did a great, great job with them."

"Thanks."

He smiled and tightened his clasp on her hand. Which made Erin wonder. "What about the part about you hitting on me?"

Mischief glimmered in his vibrant blue eyes. "Oh, that was true. It was definitely true."

Erin playfully slapped his shoulder.

He caught that hand, too. "Hey. I didn't mean literally hitting on each other. I meant hitting on each other...like this...." He used his grip to pull her onto his lap.

"Mac." Her body throbbing, Erin splayed her hands on his chest. She could feel his arousal beneath the denim of his pants.

He settled her more comfortably and threaded his hands through the hair at her nape. "I wanted you to see me as this big studly guy in a too-loose field-day T-shirt," he continued with mock seriousness.

Her nipples beading beneath her shirt, she looked down her nose at him. "The shirt wasn't all that loose."

His brow furrowed. "What do you mean?"

"Oh, come on." Erin scoffed, wanting to kiss him so badly she could taste him. "I don't have to spell it out for you."

His thumb rubbed her lower lip. "I'm afraid you do."

She exhaled sharply. "That T-shirt did great things for you—you and your powerful shoulders."

"Powerful, hmm?" He traced her upper lip, as well.

"And your rippling pecs and washboard abs." It was all she could do not to moan when his thumb slipped inside her mouth, to stroke there.

He looked pointedly down at her chest. "Your T-shirt molded to you, too." His eyes caressed what she wished his fingers would, moving slowly over her curves. "It showcased your trim waist and your gorgeous breasts." He lingered there, then ran his free hand down her hip to her thigh. "I was turned on all day."

He was still turned on, judging by the heat and strength of his arousal. However, mischief prompted her to differ. "No, you weren't."

Mac used his hand to press her closer against him. "Yeah. I was."

Lord, how she wanted him! Erin gulped, wishing they could make love right now, right here. "Maybe you are," she whispered back.

That was all it took for him to pull her all the way into his arms and deliver a long, hot kiss erotic enough to make her whimper. "Mac…" Erin quivered with need.

"We can't go inside. The kids are all sleeping. Nicholas is studying. The twins and Gavin could be home at any minute."

As if on cue, a car pulled into the lane leading up to the ranch house.

By the time Bridget and Bess got out, Erin was out of the swing and sitting opposite Mac in a chair. She'd plucked her shirt away from the telltale evidence on her chest. He'd done the same with his pants. Fortunately, it had gotten a whole lot darker since they had come out here. Although nothing, Erin decided, could hide that glint in his eyes. The look that said he wanted to make her his as soon as possible.

The twins smiled at them, as if sensing how happy it made her to be with Mac.

"What are you two doing out here?" Bridget asked, all-innocence.

Erin gestured airily. "Just relaxing a little. Talking."

"And thinking about checking out the band at the Lone Star Dance Hall," Mac said.

Erin glanced at him in surprise. "It's not a live band during the week," she felt obliged to point out. "Just a DJ. And they close at eleven, not 1:00 a.m., as they do on the weekends."

"Makes sense, it being a weeknight and all."

Bess nodded in approval. "It sounds fun."

"Heaven only knows how long it's been since you kicked up your heels like that, sis," Bridget agreed.

"Years," Erin said drily. To the point that she felt almost too old and matronly to even consider it.

"Well then, go!" Bridget said.

Bess volunteered, "We'll watch the kids."

Erin turned to Mac, hardly able to believe he'd opened

up this can of worms. "You really want to go Texas two-stepping? Now?" she asked, aghast.

Mac stood. "You bet I do."

THERE WERE MANY REASONS why they shouldn't go to the dance hall. Erin went over them as Mac drove to town. Primary among them was the fact that if she did actually go on a date with him she might lose all common sense and do something really foolish—like fall head over heels in love with him.

"Aren't you worried this is going to complicate matters?" she asked. "We're in the midst of a business deal. Or one you're attempting to make with my family, in any case." She still hadn't decided what she was going to do. Although she knew what the rest of them wanted.

He slanted her an indulgent glance. "It's customary for the sales exec to take the client out for a meal or entertainment in the midst of big deals."

Mmm-hmm. He was trying to seduce her *and* win her over to the wind farm idea.

"And exactly how many clients have you danced with?"

Comically, he clapped a hand to his heart. "You're going to dance with me? I thought we were just going to have a beer and listen to the music."

Erin told herself not to succumb to his charm. Not when her heart was on the line. "Answer the question, cowboy."

"None," he admitted with total sobriety.

Erin breathed a secret sigh of relief. "Then why me?" she asked as the scenery whizzed by.

He scoffed. "You know why."

She did and she didn't. Erin knitted her hands together in her lap. "I need you to spell it out for me."

His lips thinned. "You've had a rough few years. As, I might add, have I."

"So it's a mutual pity party?"

Mac rolled his eyes. "More like the opposite." Without warning, he steered the SUV onto the shoulder, put the vehicle in Park, released his seat belt and took her in his arms. He smoothed the hair from her face, his voice as tender as the expression on his face. "The only things I've had in my life the past couple of years are my work and my kid. That's all I've wanted. And I know you understand that."

She did.

Mac inhaled. "Then I come here…" He paused to look deep into her eyes. "And Heather and I start spending time with you and your family—and I realize how much more there is to life than what I've allowed myself." He brushed a kiss across Erin's temple, another on her cheek. "I want to have fun tonight." He gave her an extra squeeze, then kissed her sweetly once again. "And I want to have it with *you*."

IT WAS NEARLY TEN by the time they walked into the Lone Star Dance Hall, to the foot-tapping strains of "Love's Lookin' Good on You."

Her smile faded.

Mac followed the direction of Erin's gaze and saw her ex-husband seated at a table with three other gentlemen. To G.W.'s left were two county commissioners Mac had yet to get totally on board with his plan. Seated to his right was Erin's well-to-do neighbor—a single guy from Dallas who used his small, two-hundred-acre ranch as a tax shelter and weekend retreat. Drinks in front of them, they were all huddled in conversation.

"I don't believe it," Erin fumed.

Mac didn't, either. Talk about a worst-case scenario. Grasping her elbow, he leaned down to murmur in her ear, "Do you want to go somewhere else?"

The music ended.

One of G.W.'s tablemates elbowed him and nodded in their direction.

G.W. turned, made eye contact with Erin and rose.

Mac bit down on a curse as her ex ambled over.

Erin's fury intensified. "I can't believe you're here in Laramie!"

G.W. shrugged. "I got in a couple of hours ago."

She looked as if she wanted to deck him. "Just after field day ended," she pointed out.

He looked unconcerned. "The boys will understand why I wasn't there."

Erin threw up her hands in dismay. "You broke their hearts, G.W.! *Again!*"

He shook his head in wordless disagreement. Pushed on. "Have you given any more thought to Horizon Oil Company's offer?"

Erin glared. "No."

G.W.'s jaw tightened. "If you care at all about the financial future of our sons, you'll think about it," he advised. "'Cause you're still Horizon Oil's first choice, but it's not going to stay that way for long, honey. You can expect to see our formal offer tomorrow, after which you'll have five days to think about it. That's it. Then it's gone… and we'll give it to your neighbor to the south, who, by the way, is more than receptive."

G.W. tipped his hat and walked back to the table, where it seemed the party was already breaking up. Members of the group said hello to Erin and Mac as they passed on their way through the front door.

ns. Chuckling, he raised up and hooked his hands
aistband.
her help, they pushed them down to midthigh.
o feel him inside her, she cupped his legs with
nd slowly, erotically lowered her body until it
against him, but stopped short of taking him in.
oaned.
ant you," Erin whispered.
ant you, too." He undid his shirt. She spread the
hen moved forward until her breasts were nestled
ıard, hair-covered musculature of his chest. He
d and entered her with one smooth, long stroke.
gasped as the heat and strength of him invaded.
rve endings exploded with sensation. Still kissing
tly, rapaciously, she lifted herself, moving along
gth of him. Inching back down again, she took him
ıside her, then eased provocatively away.
content to let her call all the shots, Mac slid his
beneath her skirt and settled his hands on her bare
irecting the motion, the speed, he kissed and con-
, and made love to her, until there was nothing in
k Texas night but the two of them, and this mo-
n their lives.
Erin knew, whether she wanted to admit it or not,
e day Mac Wheeler had walked into her store her
d changed. Forever.

"Did you have any idea they were going to be here?" Erin asked.

Mac shook his head, taking in her miserable expression. "I wouldn't have brought you here if I had."

"Well, great." Erin sighed. "They sure threw a wrench into our evening."

"Not unless we let them," Mac retorted. Determined to recoup their earlier high spirits, he slid his hand under her elbow and led her toward the crowded bar. "Two Shiner Bock beers on draft," he told the bartender.

Erin angled her chin at him. "I thought you wanted to go."

"Not anymore." As their eyes met, chemistry sizzled between them. "We came here to enjoy ourselves tonight. That's exactly what we're going to do."

MAC WAS RIGHT, Erin thought, as the two of them clinked mugs. She couldn't change what had happened earlier in the day. She could, however, control how the rest of her evening went.

She put her lips to the frosted rim and took a sip of the cold, invigorating beer. It went down smooth and easy. And damn if it didn't feel good to be standing here, face-to-face with one of the most handsome men she had ever met. "You going to show me a good time, cowboy?" she asked with a sassy grin.

He wrapped his arm around her shoulders. "Did you ever have any doubts?"

They downed the rest of their beers, then headed for the dance floor. Together, they two-stepped their way around the floor to the beat of an old Kenny Chesney song. Swayed together to a Miranda Lambert ballad. And boogied to The Calling's "Wherever You Will Go."

There was no need to talk. No need to do anything

but dance. By the time the DJ called the last song, Erin felt lighter and happier than she had in a long, long time. Together, she and Mac headed out to the parking lot.

"Where now?" he asked.

Her spirits rose in anticipation. "There's only one place I want to go."

Half an hour later, they were back on the Triple Canyon, heading up to the bluffs. Mac parked the SUV next to the gazebo, put the windows partially down and pushed the bench seat back as far as it would go.

Cool evening air scented with sage floated over them.

His eyes trailed over her. "This could become a habit."

Erin released her seat belt, then swung herself over onto his lap, the cotton circle of her Western skirt spreading out around them. Delighting in the way they were turning each other on, she wound her arms around his neck and bent her head. "We agreed finding each other was a gift. So that means....whenever we need each other...whenever we want to feel better...we'll find a way to be together." For as long as they could. All she knew for certain was that she did not want their love affair to end.

Mac ran his fingers through her hair, rubbing the silky ends. "You do know how to sweet-talk a man," he teased.

A mixture of tenderness and affection swept through her. "I know how to sweet-talk you." She fused her lips to his, slipped her tongue into his mouth and drank in the essence of him. He reciprocated, kissing her back greedily, his lips molding to hers until she could barely breathe.

Wishing it wasn't temporary, knowing full well it was, she settled her weight over his growing hardness. He shifted against her, the fly of his jeans rubbing erotically against the most sensitive part of her. Erin let out a sigh and he did it again and again. Then reached around be-

hind her, grasping the zipper at the
bringing it down to mid-spine. Par
top, he drew it down over her shoulc
down, too. Erin pressed her lips to tl
her nipples sprang free of the consti
for his touch.

Mac chuckled and ran a hand play
elastic of her panties. "These, too," h
thrillingly rough command.

Exactly what she had been thinking!
ing, she kept her gaze on his and movec
enough to do as requested. Heart poun
back over him.

He smiled. His eyes heavy-lidded ar
her even more rapaciously.

Moving one hand up and down her
her breasts with the other, cupping the
the tender tips, until she writhed again

"Mac," she whispered desperately,
ticipation all over again.

"I know, sweetheart. I know exactl
His hand dropped to the juncture bet
Threaded through the silken curls to
sensitive spot hidden within. "What y

He moaned at the way she respon
feel so good."

She smiled as they continued to k
would feel better."

He laughed at her teasing and let he
fasten his jeans. Slip her hand inside.
was hot, damp and as ready for her a

Impatient now, Erin lifted her weig
above him, resting on her knees. "He

at his je
in the
Wit
Eager
hers,
rubbe
Mac
"
"
clot
in t
gro
F
Her
him
the
fully
N
palm
hips.
sume
the d
ment
A
that t
life h

Chapter Twelve

"What time did you get in last night?" Bridget asked the next morning when Erin walked into the kitchen to find a wholesome breakfast of oatmeal with blueberry muffins already made.

Her body still tingling from the aftereffects of the rigorous "activity" the evening before, Erin went straight for the coffeepot and poured herself a mug. "A little after one, I think." Actually, it had been more like 2:00 a.m., but who was counting?

Bess slanted her a sly glance. "You must really like him."

"Yeah, I haven't known you to pass up that ten-o'clock bedtime of yours for anyone." Bridget buttered a piping-hot muffin.

Erin looked down her nose at them. "Ha, ha."

Bess finished her oatmeal while standing with her back to the counter. "Seriously, he's a supernice guy. We hope it works out for you."

Erin scooped cereal into a bowl. She added a sprinkling of Texan pecans and dried cherries, then took a seat at the table. "There's nothing to work out. Mac's headed back to Philadelphia as soon as his business here is finished."

"Then that's reason enough to keep him hanging forever, isn't it?" Bess teased, just as Mac walked into the kitchen.

Bess looked at him in alarm. "You heard that, didn't you?"

His eyes fell on Erin. She basked in the warmth and tenderness of his gaze.

He turned back to Bess. "Yep."

Bridget lifted a brow. "And yet you're smiling."

Of course he was smiling, Erin thought a little irritably. The two of them had had a rollicking good time the evening before. First at the dance hall, then on the bluffs. Which would have all been fine if she was able to fulfill her end of their bargain, and keep her feelings and expectations within the boundaries of a consensual short-term affair. Instead, she was on the verge of falling head over heels in love with him.

"And you're frowning!" Bridget pointed out to her sister.

No surprise there, either, Erin thought, since her growing feelings for Mac were going to leave her feeling heartbroken when he inevitably left Texas. Worse, she'd have no one to blame but herself!

He edged closer, inundating her with his clean, freshly showered scent. "You feeling okay?" he asked, his gaze skimming her protectively.

Erin blushed.

Before she could say anything more, Sammy and Stevie burst into the kitchen. Heather was close behind them.

"Mom, look!" They pointed in the direction of the parking area between the house and the barns. "Dad's here! We saw his truck from the upstairs windows!"

G.W.? Erin bit down on a string of not very nice words.

The boys grabbed their ribbons from the kitchen counter and raced out the back door.

Bridget and Bess exchanged apprehensive glances. "Want us to run interference for you?" Bridget asked.

Mac seemed to be wondering the same thing.

Erin shook her head. "No…I'll handle it." She strode out the door, while Mac and Heather stayed in the kitchen with her sisters.

When she reached them, the boys were standing with G.W., eagerly expounding on field day. "See?" Stevie said. "I got this ribbon for the rope climb. I made it all the way to the top!"

"And I got this ribbon for the long jump," Sammy said. "I jumped farther than anybody in my entire class!"

G.W. smiled, pulled each boy in for an exuberant, simultaneous one-arm hug, then ruffled their hair affectionately. "That's great, boys! Really great. And I want to hear all about it in just a minute. But first I've got to talk business with your mom for a second."

He reached into his truck and emerged with a thick envelope bearing the insignia of the oil company he represented. "This is the offer. Horizon Oil wants an answer by Monday at the latest. Or I'll take their offer to your neighbor."

Not about to argue with him in front of the boys, Erin merely nodded. "Thank you for dropping this off, G.W.," she said pleasantly.

The boys, sensing she'd said all she had to say on the subject, interjected themselves excitedly once again.

"Can Dad take us to school this morning, Mom?" Sammy asked.

"It would be a good chance for us to catch up. And—" G.W. winked amenably "—for me to show them the presents I brought them." He reached into his truck once again and emerged with two pairs of inline skates the boys had been asking for. He was immediately engulfed in hugs.

"Wow, Dad!" Sammy whooped.

Stevie shouted, "You're the best!"

G.W. looked at Erin, awaiting her answer on the boys' request.

"I'd appreciate it if you would take them to school today," Erin said. They needed to be with their dad, to make up for the previous days' disappointment.

And she had matters to tend to that were best done alone.

Envelope in hand, she went back in to say a quick goodbye to everyone, including Mac and Heather, who were headed to the Montessori school. Then she left for town. En route, Erin called Travis Anderson. Luck was with her. The energy attorney had time to see her right away.

"You haven't opened the envelope," Travis observed when she handed it over.

Erin sat down at the conference table opposite him. "And I'm not going to, since there's no point. I'm not going to lease the mineral rights, no matter what the oil company is offering."

"G.W. is not going to like that."

"No kidding." They both knew how persistent her ex-husband could be when it came to a sale. "Which is why *you're* telling him no, Travis." If G.W. argued, it wouldn't matter, because she and their kids wouldn't have to hear it.

Travis made a note. "Any idea what you're going to do about the wind farm?"

Time was dwindling. Yet, unlike G.W., Mac wasn't pushing her one bit. At least not professionally.

Personally was another matter.

He was systematically tearing down the barriers between them. Opening up to her and deepening their friendship. Becoming an attentive, positive male influence for her sons, and inviting her to be the temporary stand-in-mommy for his daughter. His lovemaking had been so unforgettable she was beginning to think he might be having trouble limiting their relationship to a fling, too.

And that made things very complicated.

Aware that Travis was waiting for her answer, Erin shrugged. "If we allow anything on the property, it'll be a wind farm—and to be honest, I'm not sure my siblings and I want to do that because—"

The front door opened and slammed shut. *What the...* Erin thought, as Liz Cartwright Anderson literally stomped in. Travis's wife and law partner was nine months pregnant. Her normally impeccably groomed clothes were wrinkled, her hair was wet and it looked as if she had been crying.

"What happened?" Erin asked her long-time friend.

Liz dumped her bags on a chair in her private office and stormed into the conference room. "What else! The power went off at the ranch while I was in the shower this morning. Our well pump is electric—so of course all the water shut off immediately! I still had shampoo in my hair, so I had to get out and put a robe on and rinse my hair with water from the jugs we've been keeping around for emergencies." She blew out an exasperated breath. "I waited thirty minutes, thinking surely the power would come back on again. It didn't. Then, of course, I couldn't dry my hair or iron my blouse...."

Travis swallowed nervously. "Sweetheart...I—"

She lifted a staying hand. "Don't you *dare* try to placate me, Travis. I'm sick and tired of the rolling blackouts." Her lip trembled. "What are we going to do when the baby comes? We can't have a newborn and no power. And what about Great-grandmother Tillie and my grandmother, Faye-Elizabeth? They can't get overheated, either, and with the hottest summer on record predicted, coming soon…" She burst into a flood of tears so wrenching Erin wanted to cry, too.

"Hey, now." Travis circled the table and embraced his wife lovingly, damp hair and all. "I know it's been tough, and it will be for a while longer, but it's not going to go on forever. The county commissioners are going to figure out how to deal with the power shortage next week."

"Is that why you're here?" Liz turned to Erin, blotting her eyes in relief. "Because you've decided to make a deal with North Wind Energy?"

Guilt flooded through Erin. She knew if she said yes, and the wind farm was built, the blackouts in the far-flung areas of the county would stop. Unfortunately, her desire to help her community did not trump her familial obligations.

Erin shook her head. "I don't know what I'm going to do."

Travis gently explained to his wife, "Erin's here because she wants me to represent her and her family and turn down G.W.'s offer in a way he and the oil company will understand is final. So he won't keep pestering her and putting her in a bad light with her kids by refusing to do business that would benefit him."

Liz smiled sympathetically and eased into a chair. "Travis is good at helping ladies in distress." She settled into her seat with a wince. "And I don't know what in the world is wrong with me today, anyway. I'm not usually anywhere near so emotional— Oh! What in the world…"

They all looked down.

Liquid was running off the seat of Liz's leather chair, down her legs, pooling on the floor. "I think my water just broke!" She looked at Erin, a little dazed, and a lot confused. "Is that what happened?" she asked, needing—wanting—confirmation in the way that new moms-to-be relied on their friends who had already been through it.

It certainly appeared to be, Erin thought, overcome by sentimentality. Having a baby was one of the biggest days of a woman's life. At least it had been for her.

Erin stood and helped ease Liz out of her chair. "Travis, I think our business is going to have to wait." She made sure Liz was steady and Travis was right there to take over. "You have a wife to get to the hospital, and a new baby to bring into the world." Abruptly, Erin choked up. Which was no surprise. Newborn babies always brought out bittersweet tears in her.

Every bit as action-oriented as usual, Travis ushered his wife toward the door. "When's the response due?"

Erin walked into the break room to get a fistful of paper towels. "Monday."

He nodded. "I'll get to it over the weekend, I promise."

SEVERAL HOURS LATER, Mac settled more comfortably in the passenger seat of his rented SUV, his laptop beside him, cell phone set to Speaker, a satellite map of this part of Laramie County open in front of him. It was a beautiful May day. Not too hot yet. A nice breeze blew through the open windows, and wildflowers were still blooming. From on top of the bluffs, he could see not just Erin's ranch, but those of adjoining properties, and the current power station, too. Although he could easily have gone back to the ranch house to check in with his superior, he had decided to come here to discuss business.

"I reviewed your request regarding your personal situation last night," Louise told him over the phone. "I can sell it to my bosses, but in return we are going to want something from you first."

Mac had expected as much. "The wind farm in Laramie County."

"That's got to happen," Louise stated briskly. "How close are you?"

Close enough to start making plans to drastically improve my life. "I talked to two other ranchers this morning," Mac said. "Jeremy Carrigan and his wife are ready to sign, although topographically their land is less than ideal, and they have only a quarter of the land we're going to need. Matt and Emmett Briscoe are leaning our way."

Mac figured once the two Briscoe men saw all the numbers and visited the wind farm on Saturday, they'd be convinced, too. After all, the family would still have plenty of room to run their cattle on their massive fifty-thousand-acre property. And the area they were talking about was rocky, with thin, sparse soil. The only difficulty was that it was at the far western edge of Laramie County, which meant either a second power plant would have to be built, or an awful lot of line run to the existing one, a fact that would up the cost to North Wind Energy and the county dramatically.

"What about Erin Monroe? What is she saying on behalf of her family?"

Mac knew the Triple Canyon Ranch was still the first choice of everyone involved, including the county commissioners ready to vote on the project. Had he been focused strictly on business, he would have made the deal with her by now.

He hadn't. Which was ironic. He had always criticized his parents for not doing what they needed to do to get ahead, even when things were within their grasp. They had chosen family time together over furthering their educations after hours. More time off over increased pay and responsibility. And his mom had continued the pattern even after his dad died, and they were barely making ends meet. Mac had taken the opposite route. Experienced great professional and financial success because of it. And now…

Now he was on the fence, just as Erin was.

Wondering what was right. What would really make him and everyone close to him happy.

"Hello? Mac? Are you still there?" Louise shouted into the phone.

"Yeah. Sorry. I was distracted by an email that just came through," Mac fibbed.

"About Ms. Monroe…" Louise asked, in a more normal tone.

"I haven't pushed her."

"Because…" Louise prodded.

Because I care about what she thinks and feels and needs and wants. Mac cleared his throat. "It's an emotional subject with her. As I've told you, Texans are very sentimental about their land." *And she lost her only daughter there. Lived there as a kid. Raised her siblings there, after her parents' deaths.* That stuff shouldn't matter to him, but it did, just as she did.

"It's your job to make Ms. Monroe see the value of clean energy and cold hard cash. Besides, I thought that property wasn't being used agriculturally."

"It's not, but it's still been in the family for generations, which is why I've been pitching to other landowners. I'm thinking if maybe more than one person sacrificed his or her ranch for the greater good of the community, or was just financially ready to get out, it would be an easier sell to the county commissioners."

"Not if it's more expensive to build, it won't. In this day and age it *always* comes down to the bottom line."

Did it? Before he'd arrived in Laramie, Mac would have thought that to be true.

"You're not getting emotionally involved in this situation, are you?" Louise asked bluntly.

Caught off guard, Mac scrambled for cover. "Like I told you earlier, Texans are a breed unto themselves..."

"Yes, I know," Louise repeated with a sigh. "They're strong and independent. Kind and neighborly, right down to their bones. I get it, Mac, I really do. But what *you* need to understand is that in order to secure that cushy financial future you so desperately want for yourself and Heather, you're going to have to do whatever it takes to close this deal with Laramie County." There was a long pause. "And from what I've been able to see, that means convincing Ms. Monroe that selling out to North Wind Energy is in her best interest."

"MAC'S NOT GOING TO BE here for dinner tonight?" Nicholas asked, obviously disappointed.

Erin shook her head. Heather was playing outside with Sammy and Stevie. "He has a dinner meeting with the head of the Laramie County Planning and Zoning Department."

Nicholas frowned. "He didn't say anything about it this morning."

"I think it just came up."

"It's going to be weird when he and Heather aren't with us anymore, you know?"

Did she ever. "I think we'll all miss them."

His expression wistful, Nicholas nodded at the trio playing outside. "Seeing them together like that, it's kind of like when Angelica was alive, don't you think?"

Realizing how much her littlest brother was missing their angel, too, Erin put a comforting arm around his shoulders. "I agree."

Nicholas exhaled roughly. "Does that seem disloyal to you? Like we're forgetting her?"

"Not anymore. At first it did, though." Erin fell silent as she struggled to put her feelings into words. "Now, it's sort of like Heather was sent here by Angelica, to remind us that there are still plenty of children to love in this world…and that our love for Angelica is in no way diminished by us caring for someone else."

He nodded, his eyes moist. Without warning, he broke into sobs. Startled, Erin took him into her arms. She forgot sometimes how hard it was for everyone in the family, not just her.

"Sorry, sis…" he choked out.

Erin hugged him all the tighter. "It's okay, Nick. Just let it out." Tears streamed down her own face, as well. "Let it go…."

They stood that way awhile, their bodies shaking with shared tears. Eventually, as it always did, the storm passed.

And that was when Erin looked up and saw Mac framed in the kitchen doorway, his eyes wet, too.

MAC KNEW HE SHOULDN'T have intruded on what was a private family moment. But when he'd heard Erin talking to Nicholas, he'd been transfixed.

Humiliated to be caught crying in front of another guy, Nicholas rubbed his eyes, mumbled an excuse and rushed from the room.

Erin moved blindly past Mac to the fridge. Obviously embarrassed, she worked to compose herself, too. "I thought you weren't going to be here for dinner." She opened up the crisper and pulled out the makings for salad.

Mac hated to admit how much a home the ranch had become, or how good it felt to be here. He was almost glad there'd been another hitch in business. "My dinner partner canceled on me."

"Oh?" Still not looking at him directly, Erin closed the door with her hip.

Mac wished he could just say to hell with everything, take her in his arms...let the rest of the world go away.

How crazy was that?

Aware that Erin was still waiting to hear why the dinner was canceled, Mac said, "That particular commissioner had second thoughts about meeting with me. Seems Prairie Natural Gas has been working hard to convince him that the most practical alternative would be to stay with the same fuel and simply expand the capacity of the existing power plant."

Erin's eyes shone sympathetically. She might not want the turbines on her property, but she did want more power. "There's nothing you can do?"

Mac walked over to snag a carrot slice. "I talked him into going on the bus tour on Saturday."

Erin handed Mac a radish, too. "How many people are signed up?"

Feeling right at home in her kitchen, he settled next to her and watched her work. "Right now, we've got two buses at capacity, and we're working on filling a third."

"Would you like me and the kids to go, too?"

As she moved, he was inundated with the lilac scent of her hair and skin. And treated to an up-close view of her soft lips and very pretty green eyes.

Damn, but he liked being with her. Anywhere, any way, anytime. He struggled to handle the unexpected wave of sentimentality. "You're up for watching all three of them all day?" This didn't necessarily mean anything. She was probably just being nice. It didn't mean she was going to say yes. To him. To his deal.

Oblivious to his thoughts, Erin focused on slicing a tomato. "It won't be a problem, especially if I can get Nicholas and the twins to go, too."

It was beginning to sound like a family affair. And that made him feel as if he and Heather were part of her family. A dangerous proposition for someone trying to keep his business acumen intact.

"Are you that interested?" Mac asked, blunt to a fault. Then, seeing the surprise on her face, he quipped, "Or just looking for something different to fill a Saturday?"

Erin hesitated in a way that let him know she was as conflicted as he was. About damn near everything. Except the lust. The lust they agreed was strong and intact and not likely to ever go away. Which made standing here trying to be the perfect gentleman extremely difficult. "Just a little friendly support," she said finally.

"Well, don't get too friendly," Gavin remarked, coming in on the heels of their conversation. As usual, he was still clad in his blue hospital scrubs, and looked dog-tired. And, as usual, he saw what was going on between Mac and Erin, and that in turn made him extra protective of his sister.

Gavin reached past Erin and helped himself to a slice of cucumber. He shot Mac a look that reminded him that Gavin had already warned him away.

To no avail.

He and Erin couldn't put whatever this was aside.

They had tried.

But not enough, according to Erin's brother.

"Mac's leaving soon, remember? To go back to Philadelphia." Gavin snatched a piece of green pepper. "Or he will be, as soon as the county either approves or votes down his proposal."

Erin turned on her brother. "I thought as a physician that you would be in favor of such an environmentally friendly way of providing energy," she said.

Gavin stared at Mac. "I'm in favor of anything and everything that's good for this family. What I'm not so wild about are so-called friends just blowing through town."

Ouch. "Don't mince words on my account," Mac drawled, losing his East Coast accent for a put-on West Texas drawl meant to irritate.

"I wasn't planning to," Gavin retorted.

Erin looked at them both. "Guys..." she warned, as the three youngest came trooping in the back door.

"We're hungry!" Sammy announced.

"Yeah, when's dinner?" Stevie demanded.

Heather skidded to a halt beside them. She was wearing the cowgirl boots and hat Erin had helped her pick out, and was as hot and sweaty and dusty as the boys. Sandwiched between the two little athletes, she had a grin that spread from ear to ear. "Daddy," she said, not for the first time, "can we stay here forever and ever? Because I need some brothers and this ranch is the bestest place ever!"

Sensing a storm coming on if he was as honest as he needed to be, Mac hunkered down so they could talk face-to-face. "I'm glad you like it, honey, but it's not that simple."

"Yeah, it is." Stevie piped up with perfect elementary school logic. "We could be brothers and sisters. And Heather and you could stay here with us from now on. All you have to do, Mac, is marry my mom and we'll be all set."

Chapter Thirteen

The kids kept lobbying for marriage between Mac and Erin all through dinner. They were still chattering about it when they were tucked in, no matter how many times and ways the embarrassed two of them tried to explain it just wasn't in the cards.

Fortunately, right after that, a series of phone calls from interested parties eager to sign up for the Saturday bus trip kept Mac busy. Erin, glad for a respite, and needing time to think, turned in before ten.

Sleep, however, proved to be elusive. A bleary-eyed Erin was still ruminating on how to put a stop to the innocent matchmaking—and keep her own private wishes under wraps—the next morning, when she was getting ready to take Heather to the Mother's Day tea.

"It's still not right, Daddy. It looks awful!" Heather's petulant cry echoed through the Triple Canyon ranch house.

"Heather, come back here!" Mac called. "I can fix it!"

"No, you can't! I want Erin to help me!"

Footsteps pounded down the hallway. The door to Erin's bedroom was thrown open and Heather appeared in the doorway. Her curly blond hair, always a challenge, was particularly wonky this morning.

Mac showed up a minute later, hairbrush in one hand, flower-decorated headband in the other.

Heather stopped beside Erin, who was in the process of putting on earrings, and looked into the mirror. The child's lower lip thrust out in dismay.

"It's really not that bad," Mac said, coming up behind them.

There was no use pretending. Heather would see right though him. "Yes, it is," Erin said, fingering the frizzy curls, which were smashed down on one side and whipping out wildly on the other. "The bad news is my hair looked just like that when I got out of bed this morning." It was the spring heat and humidity. "The good news is I can tame your curls, just the way I tamed mine."

Heather turned around. Looking cute as could be, she placed her hands on her hips. "You need to leave, Daddy. This is just for us girls."

Mac handed over the hair tools and sent Erin a look of gratitude. "I'll be downstairs waiting," he promised.

He slipped out of the room.

Unable to help but think of the many times she had done the same for Angelica, Erin patted her bed. "Why don't you have a seat up here," she said.

She slipped into her bathroom and returned with a bottle of leave-in conditioner. Rubbing some between her palms, and sitting down behind Heather, Erin used her fingers to work it through the frizzy curls. Magically, they sprang into sleek uniform spirals. The pleasant scent of the hair product filled the room.

Erin used a wide-toothed pick to fluff up the curls, then slid the headband Mac had brought into place. "Now, go have a look," she urged.

Heather climbed down from the bed, walked over to

the full-length mirror and smiled at her reflection. "Now my hair looks pretty," she declared.

"*You* look pretty," Erin said.

"So do you," a deep male voice said.

Erin looked over. Freshly shaved, Mac stood framed in the doorway. Dressed in khakis, a light blue button-up shirt and Western boots, he looked handsome and at ease. Their eyes met and Erin's heart took a little leap.

He shrugged. "Sorry. It was so quiet up here, I had to come and check. I'm glad I did." He let out a low wolf whistle, as his glance took in their pretty flowered sundresses, strappy sandals and artfully arranged blond curls. "You are two very gorgeous ladies."

Heather grinned. "Erin fixed my hair, just like a mommy would."

The mommy that they all knew she no longer had, but had begun to want fiercely, nonetheless.

"And I sat nice and still for her, just like a daughter would."

The daughter Erin no longer had—and missed just as desperately. "You sure did," she praised, her voice husky.

"Well, I think both your efforts paid off," Mac declared, strolling closer to gaze into Erin's eyes.

Two more males appeared in the doorway. Sammy elbowed Stevie. "See, I told you they were going to be in love."

"Yeah, yeah, I know. And next thing they'll be kissing," Stevie continued informatively. "And after that…"

Mac and Erin winced in unison.

"…married."

MAC SETTLED THE BOYS in his rental, while Erin belted Heather into her SUV. He met her midway between the two vehicles. "You going to be okay this morning?"

They both knew why she might not be.

Erin swallowed the knot of emotion that had been in her throat all morning. Glancing at Heather, who was practically jittery with excitement, her courage rose. "I will." *But thanks for caring so much.*

He squeezed her hand, intuitively understanding, as always, so much more about her than she had ever dreamed possible. "Thanks for doing this."

"Thanks for taking my boys to school."

Heather chattered nonstop on the drive into town. "My best friends at school are William and Nathan. But I like Tamara, too. And Liza. And Roger..."

As they passed ranch after picturesque ranch, Erin heard about all the activities at the Montessori school. The sheer wealth of information made her realize that up until now, Mac's daughter's attention had always been divided among the family. This was the first time the two of them had been completely alone. It was amazing how at ease they were with one another, how right this felt.

She hadn't enjoyed such rapport with a little girl since her own daughter had died. A fact that made the morning all the more bittersweet.

Erin pushed away the twinge of guilt she felt for letting someone else take Angelica's place. Her daughter would want her to be happy.

Erin caught Heather's bright-eyed glance in her rearview mirror. The sight of her, so pretty and poised, brought forth a landslide of tenderness inside her. Erin clung to that feeling and returned her attention to the road. "So what's your favorite thing every day in school?"

Heather thought hard. "I like recess," she said finally.

Erin laughed. "I used to love recess, too."

"Especially when the boys chase me and the other girls."

Erin had liked that, too. "What else?" she prompted.

"I like making presents, like what I made for you, only I can't tell you what that is, on account of it's s'posed to be a secret."

"Well, I'm sure I will love it, whatever it is," Erin murmured as they reached the school. She guided her SUV into a parking space and cut the motor. Getting out of the car, she opened the rear door. "Ready to rock and roll?"

Heather paused, her hand on the clasp of her safety belt. Her glance fell to some of the other children going into the school for the mother-student tea. Her expression sober, she said, "You have to be my real mommy today. It can't just be pretend," she warned urgently. "Because no one else is going to be pretending."

Erin knew there were several other "stand-ins" attending the event with students. In one case, an aunt. Another, a family friend. In yet another, a grandmother. Mac had explained as much to Heather the night before; she hadn't accepted it then and wasn't about to now.

So Erin didn't even try offering facts or logic, since it wasn't likely to comfort Mac's daughter in any case. Instead, she slid into the backseat, wreathed her arms around Heather's slender shoulders and pressed a kiss into her hair. "I'll be your real mommy today," she promised.

Heather leaned into Erin's touch and breathed an enormous sigh of relief. The affection between them was so strong and real it nearly brought tears to Erin's eyes. "Ready now?" she asked thickly.

Heather nodded. Trembling slightly, she let go of her lap belt and climbed out of the car, her pink backpack in tow. Erin reached for her, and the two of them walked into the building hand in hand.

MAC KNEW HE SHOULD LET the chips fall where they may this morning. It wasn't as if he was invited; dads had been specifically excluded from this Mother's Day school event. Besides, Heather had vehemently vetoed his attendance from the first moment the tea was brought up—despite the fact that he was more than willing to fill in for her mother. Because the truth was, he was both mom and dad to her, and had been for two years now.

Just as Erin was both mom and dad to her boys the majority of the time.

They were accustomed to the roles assigned. They accepted the unfairness of it all.

Yet when he had watched Erin help Heather with her hair this morning, he'd had to admit that, as much as he did and as hard as he tried, he still wasn't giving his daughter everything she needed. Or wanted.

Heather needed a mom in her life.

She needed Erin.

But there were roadblocks to that, too.

First and foremost, the underlying anxiety both females had exhibited in their own quiet ways.

Which was why he had pushed back another appointment he needed to keep, right after he had dropped Sammy and Stevie off at Laramie Elementary, and headed on over to the Montessori school.

The school secretary understood his concern, even as she cautioned, "There won't be a chair for you at any of the tables."

"I don't really want to be visible," Mac admitted. "That would embarrass Heather. I just want to be available to come to the rescue in case there's some sort of meltdown."

"I understand. Situations like this can be tricky. Here's what we'll do.... The event is being held in the cafeteria. You can stand backstage, in the wings, while the student

sandwiches for all. Plus…look what I got." Erin held out her wrist for his inspection. On it was a rainbow-colored beaded bracelet with a heart-shaped silver clasp. "Heather made it for me."

"Beautiful. Just like you."

Mac bent his head and kissed Erin. She kissed him back, taking her time with that, too, until they were once again very much in sync.

Deciding she'd done enough for the day on his custom boots—which were on track to be finished in time for the county commissioners meeting—Erin took him by the hand and led him out of the shop, toward the house. At times like this she almost felt married to him. Which was ridiculous. They weren't even really dating, although they were lovers. That much was obvious.

"So." Aware her spirits were soaring as much as her pulse, and that maybe she was starting to depend on him a little too much for comfort, she decided to put on the brakes. "How was the rest of your day?" There. That sounded casual. Like the kind of thing they could both easily walk away from, as planned.

"Good. Busy." The phone buzzed in his pocket, and Mac frowned at the interruption.

Knowing all he had at stake, Erin advised, "Better get it."

Mac took the call. "Wheeler. Yeah. Absolutely." He smiled and gave her a thumbs-up. "There's still room on the sixth bus for four more."

There were *six* buses now, all headed north?

Apparently so, Erin deduced, as Mac finished that call and then took the one after, and the one after that.

She pointed at the fridge, indicating he should help himself, blew him a kiss and then, wary of their early morning and long, long day ahead, headed upstairs to bed.

"AMAZING, ISN'T IT?" Nicholas remarked the following afternoon, as the three hundred citizens gazed out at the North Wind Energy wind farm on the Panhandle.

It was roughly two-thirds the size of the one being proposed for their county. The turbines stretched out across the plain as far as the eye could see, in line after line.

"It's oddly peaceful," Bridget said.

"Not to mention environmentally friendly," Nicholas added.

Heather pointed at the windmills and bragged to Stevie and Sammy, "That's what my daddy sells to people. They make 'lectricity."

"Awesome!" Sammy and Stevie said in unison.

At the center of the group, Mac was taking questions, explaining the specifics of how things worked, how long it took to install, and so on.

The PTA president came over to Erin. "Well, I'm sold. I'm so glad your family is allowing this to happen on Monroe land."

The twins' brows furrowed in unison.

Erin lifted a hand, indicating she would handle this. "Like I've said before…let's not get ahead of ourselves here, Marybeth. Nothing has been officially decided yet."

The woman winked. "That's it. You go, girl. Negotiate the best price you possibly can for your family. Just know that the community is solidly behind you!"

And so it went for the rest of the trip, during the tour of the power plant supplied by the wind farm, and the long bus ride back to Laramie.

By the time they finally got back to the ranch late Saturday evening, Erin was completely overwhelmed by the pressure, guilt and indecision.

Bridget and Bess took one look at her and knew she needed a break. "Why don't you two let us put the kids to bed?" Bess asked. She waved Mac and Erin back out the door they had just come through. "Why don't you-all go relax somewhere."

"We do have to feed the horses," Erin said.

"Got that covered, sis," Nicholas said.

Another look of heightened concern passed among the three siblings, and suddenly Erin knew. "What's going on?" Mac asked as they walked back out the door to the porch.

She settled on the bench swing, her mood taking another downward spiral. "They're worried about me."

Mac sat beside her and draped his arm along the back of the swing.

Erin settled against him, felt the welcoming heat of his body. Right or wrong, at this moment she needed Mac. "Tomorrow is Mother's Day." Which he knew. What he didn't was…

Erin swallowed hard and kept her eyes on the soft glow of the moonlight flooding the yard. Quietly, she said, "The second anniversary of Angelica's death is also tomorrow. We've got plans to go to the cemetery and visit her grave site, as a family. So…" She breathed around the sudden clenching in her chest. "My guess is they're probably wondering if I'm going to lose it."

Mac tightened his hold on her. "Is that what's happened in the past?"

The tightness in Erin's chest became a pain around her heart. Tears blurred her eyes. "It's hard."

He turned to take her all the way into his arms, hugged her fiercely. This was the place where people usually offered up lots of platitudes in consolation. Mac did none of that. Instead, he asked, "Want Heather and me to go with you?"

Erin did, but Heather was just a little girl….

Mac pulled back far enough to be able to look into Erin's eyes. "She understands grief. We've visited her mom's grave site together, too. She knows it can be healing." He gently touched Erin's face. "But in the end it's whatever you want..." he proclaimed softly.

There was no question there, Erin knew. No question about what she needed. Blinking back tears, she told him, "What I want is for you and Heather to go with us." *What I want is for all of us to be together, to be a family.*

Chapter Fourteen

"Erin?" Bess called from downstairs at nine the next morning. "Phone for… Oh. Okay," she continued, before Erin could reach her. "Yes. I'll tell her."

With one hand on the banister, Erin stopped to put on her flats.

"That was G.W. He won't be able to make it this morning."

Big surprise, Erin thought.

"He said he'll go by later to pay his respects," her sister added.

Erin nodded. She hadn't really expected her ex to go with them. To her knowledge, he hadn't visited their daughter's grave since the day they'd buried her. The grief was just too much for him.

"You okay?" Bridget asked, as Erin joined her at the bottom of the steps.

She nodded.

Sammy and Stevie came down the stairs next. They were dressed as Erin had requested, in their good shirts, khaki pants and boots. Heather followed in one of her frilly pink dresses and pink cowgirl boots. Mac was right behind her. In a sage-green shirt, black slacks and the ready-made boots she'd sold him, he looked debonair as ever.

Nicholas and Gavin arrived from the kitchen, where they'd been having breakfast. "Everybody ready?" Erin asked.

There were nods all around.

"Then let's go," she said.

At Erin's request—she wanted some time alone with her sons in case they had anything on their minds—they drove out to the cemetery in a four-car caravan. The twins in one, Erin and the boys in another, Mac and Heather in a third. Nicholas rode with Gavin in his pickup truck.

"I like having Mac and Heather with us," Sammy said after a while.

"It's kind of like having a dad again," Stevie agreed, happiness radiating in his voice. "Not that he is our dad, but..." He shot Erin an apprehensive glance. "You know what I mean."

She nodded, not the least bit upset. "I do." It felt good having a man she could count on around. Good to have Mac stand by her. As a lover, as a friend. And maybe, if she was very lucky one day, something more...

"Do you think he might decide to stay here in Texas?" Sammy asked. "People do that all the time, you know. They decide they like Laramie and buy a house here and stuff. Even if it's just for weekends."

Erin knew that was true. Texans were big on having rural retreats. Whether in the form of a ranch or simply a cabin somewhere didn't seem to matter. Everyone liked the great outdoors.

"I don't know, honey." Erin's heart lurched as the Laramie Memorial Cemetery came into view. "Mac's home and work are in Philadelphia—and that's a long way from here—so I wouldn't count on it."

"But he and Heather could come and visit us, couldn't he? Anytime they wanted? Maybe vacation here?" Stevie asked.

Erin smiled. "We will certainly tell them our door is always open, and to come back as often as they like. How's that?"

In her rearview mirror, she saw the boys nod enthusiastically.

Erin followed the twins down the winding drive to the Monroe family section.

The sun was shining in a clear blue sky overhead. The temperature was warm and temperate. A soft flower-scented breeze was blowing. Just as it had been the day they'd laid Angelica to rest,

Erin gathered with her family around the headstone. They joined hands and said a brief, heartfelt prayer. "Amen." The sound of their mingled voices echoed through the peaceful tranquility of the morning.

It was odd, Erin thought, to feel so comforted by such a simple ritual. Odd to feel so close to her daughter, here and now.

And just that suddenly, grief welled.

Bridget let out a sob. Bess clapped a hand over her mouth. Tears flowed. Sammy and Stevie broke free of Erin to engulf a tearful Heather in a hug. The next thing Erin knew, Mac's arms were around her, holding her close. His tears were wet on her face. Hers dampened his shirt. Needing him as never before, she clasped him tightly, as Nicholas and Gavin hugged their sisters. And the heartbreak of loss led to an even greater outpouring of love.

Eventually, though, they all got hold of themselves.

One by one the tears stopped...and tremulous smiles slowly emerged.

Before long, everyone became aware of the sound of the birds in the trees, and the warmth of the Texas breeze on that peaceful Sunday morning.

"Mom. What about the balloons?" Sammy asked.

"Yeah, we got to send them up to Angelica in heaven," Stevie insisted.

"I have them," Erin said. She went over to the twins' sedan, where she'd put a box containing a dozen pastel balloons with strings. She also had paper, pens and tape for everyone.

"We get to write a message to Angelica," Sammy explained to Heather.

"Yeah, and we're gonna send her some of our ribbons from track-and-field day, too," Stevie said. "So she can have some, too, even though she didn't get to participate."

Touched, Erin said, "That's really nice, boys. I know she'll like that and be proud of you both."

Heather pulled the pink ribbon headband from her hair. "Daddy, can I send this? 'Cause Angelica might not have one up there."

Mac hugged his daughter. "I think that's a great idea."

The next few minutes were busy ones, as messages were written and secured, one by one, to the strings on the balloons. Finally, they all were done. Everyone held their balloons. "Ready?" Erin asked, and they all let go at once.

The balloons drifted upward in a rainbow of pastel colors. Scattering, catching on the breeze, they went higher and higher until they disappeared from view.

Silence fell.

Erin was at peace once again. And so, it seemed, was everyone else.

Mac came over and caught her hand in his. This time he didn't let go.

"I VOTE FOR A PICNIC," Bess said, as they headed en masse toward their vehicles.

Erin was surprised Mac still had her palm clasped tightly in his, but was no more ready to let go of him than he was of her. She needed him today. And he seemed to need her, as well.

"How about on the bluffs?" Bridget asked. "We haven't been there as a family in forever. Not since, well…" She paused, looked at Erin as if for permission. "Don't you think it's time?"

Erin blushed as she thought about the wild pleasure she and Mac had enjoyed on the bluffs. It had always been her favorite place on the ranch. Now even more so. The irreverent grin tugging at the corners of his mouth said Mac was thinking the same. "Okay with me," he said with a shrug.

The little kids let out a whoop that was somehow appropriate to the situation. One, Erin knew, that Angelica would have participated in, as well. "Then let's go," she said. "I'll get the food and—"

"No, you won't," Bess said.

"The rest of us will handle it," Bridget promised. "You and Mac go on up to the bluffs and relax. This is Mother's Day. You deserve a break, and Mac—we're relying on you to see that she gets it."

"THAT WAS QUITE A BIT of matchmaking back there," Erin said forty-five minutes later, when she and Mac got out of his SUV and walked toward the pavilion. "Do you mind?"

"No." He ran a hand up and down her back. "We haven't had very much time alone lately."

She met his gaze. "I've missed you."

He bent his head and kissed her warmly. "I've missed you." He wrapped his arms around her, and Erin felt a familiar peace steal over her. They stayed like that for a while.

"I wish things were different," she said finally. She gave herself up to him, savoring their closeness. "I wish we'd met years ago. When we both were free."

In answer, Mac tugged her even closer and ruffled her hair. "Then there'd be no Heather and Sammy and Stevie and Angelica."

Erin smiled at his practical nature. "No divorce or loss of spouse. No business complications or far-flung jobs and residences keeping us apart."

He kissed her temple. "I thought we were keeping this light and easy."

She sucked in an uneven breath. "I'm trying."

He drew back to search her eyes. "But it's a fruitless effort."

Erin shrugged and couldn't look away. "Whenever I'm near you like this, this is all I want." She stood on tiptoe and lightly pressed her lips to his. "You're all I want."

He shook his head with a mixture of lust and something else…something far deeper…in his blue eyes. "You're all I want, too," he told her huskily, kissing her again, even more passionately this time.

When at last Mac pulled back, he looked down at her as if memorizing her features for all time. "We need to talk," he told her in a low voice. "About us. About everything. But it's going to have to wait until after the business side is concluded."

Erin inhaled a shaky breath. Was it possible Mac was as deeply enamored of her as she was of him? As reluctant to let go? "Agreed."

His expression implacable, Mac said, "I don't want anything—especially business—getting in the way."

Erin squeezed his hands. She didn't, either.

"YOU MUST HAVE HAD a great Mother's Day," Darcy remarked the next morning, when Erin showed up at the store.

Erin had never been good at hiding her feelings. Still, it would be good to hear what her friend was thinking. "How do you figure that?" she asked curiously.

"You're smiling from ear to ear." Darcy keyed her employee code into the cash register. "Seriously, it was okay this year?"

Erin walked around, turning on lights. "More than okay." Briefly, she related what had happened the day before, culminating with the heartfelt gifts and cards her family—and Heather—had given her to celebrate her special day.

Darcy nodded. "What about Mac?"

He'd given her the best gift of all. Peace. The feeling of being cared for, the hope that what they shared would one day turn into love. If it hadn't done so already. Erin knew, when it came to her feelings, she was close to the point of no return.

"I'm not Mac's mother."

Darcy coughed. "Clearly."

"Or his wife." Although she'd like to be.

Whoa! Where had *that* thought come from?

"Hmm. Well, I've got a message for you. Travis Anderson called and wanted to tell you he sent you an email. He wants you to vet the letter to Horizon Oil Company before he sends it off. And he'd prefer to do that as soon as possible, since he and Liz are in the throes of baby-girl bliss." Darcy stopped and clapped a hand over her mouth. "I'm sorry. I—" Like everyone else who knew her, Darcy had refrained from talking about other couples with precious little girls, for fear of what emotions it would conjure up for Erin.

Erin's heart skipped a beat when he reached into his pants pocket and pulled out a small, navy-blue velvet box. "You didn't have to d-do this," she stammered.

He smiled. "I think I did. You're such a good mom and you've been so kind to Heather and to me. I wanted to give you something for Mother's Day, too. But I wanted to do it in private."

And this was, Erin knew, the first chance they'd had to be really and truly alone in days.

With trembling fingers, she undid the white satin ribbon and opened the lid. Inside was a heart-shaped gold locket on a chain. On the front were engraved the words *Light of My Life.* On the back were the dates of Angelica's birth and death. Inside were two photos, one of Angelica as a newborn, the other taken toward the end, when she was still alert and happy. "Oh, Mac..."

He cupped Erin's shoulders with his palms and locked eyes with her. "I bought this for you because I get it. You're always going to be Angelica's mom. I understand you wanting to hang on to that," he said with heartfelt poignancy. "I don't want you to forget her, either."

With tears obscuring her vision, Erin dived into his arms and wreathed her arms about his neck, the locket still clutched in her hand. "I love you," she said before she could stop herself. "I love you so much."

His answering smile was slow and sure. He threaded his hands through her hair and bent his head. Always more a man of action than words, he clasped her to him. His lips met hers in a scorching kiss that was so deep and romantic it fulfilled every sexual fantasy she had ever had. Erin gave her feelings free rein in return. Not stopping, even when he swept her up in his arms and carried her to her bedroom.

There, the passion quickly built to a fever pitch. His

hands were as busy as hers, stroking and loving, taking each other to ecstasy.

Mac slid between her legs. Erin opened herself up to him and he thrust deep inside. Control eluded them. Their breathing came in a rush, and the connection between them kicked into high gear, until at last they found the hot, shimmering release they craved.

Mac collapsed on top of her. Then he shifted, so she was on top, her head pillowed on his shoulder, his arms tight around her.

She'd barely recovered when he made love to her again.

And then one more time.

And only when they were both exhausted, their bodies sated, did he raise himself on his elbow and stare down in her face.

She could tell. Whatever this was—it was serious.

Intent, focused, he said softly, "About what you said earlier..."

That she'd admitted she loved him.

And he...hadn't.

Her spirits crashing as swiftly as they had soared, Erin flashed a casual "everything's all right" smile and got up to find her clothing. Her gaze still averted, she slipped on her panties and bra, then found the locket she'd been too busy to put on, and had as a consequence left on the bedside table.

Please don't let me ruin this when we have so little time left, and please, please, please, don't let him tell me he doesn't feel the same. Because, heaven knows, there are some things better left unspoken.

Erin bent her head, then turned her back to him so he could assist her with the clasp of the necklace. "Forget it, Mac," she told him kindly.

I was a fool.

"I can't," he said just as gently.

Erin knew he was waiting for her to turn and look him in the eye. She shrugged again. "I got carried away."

Mac came up behind her, his big body emanating heat and desire. "We tend to do that a lot, don't we?" he teased, as he reached up to assist.

When he had a hold of the chain, Erin lifted her hair. She shut her eyes briefly. The backs of his fingers brushed the nape of her neck. She worked to affect a light attitude, even as her heart pounded in her chest. "We certainly do." Just now, she'd been more "carried away" than she had in her entire life. To the point her body was still tingling. And his was likely doing the same.

But passion and tenderness, understanding and friendship, weren't the same as love. He knew that. Accepted it.

Did she?

Mac fastened the clasp. Savoring the feel of him so close to her, Erin held the locket, which was now pressed against her chest.

Gently, he turned her around, looked deep into her eyes. "And I do want to have that conversation," he told her quietly, meaningfully.

Just not now.

Erin wanted to tell Mac it was okay. That this wasn't a conversation they ever had to have. Or in other words, just because she was a romantic fool didn't mean he had to be, too. They could continue on just as they were, as they had previously agreed they would. As the unexpected gift they were to each other, as lovers and very good friends.

They could feel like a family when they needed to be. And go their separate ways when they didn't.

Erin opened her mouth, not sure how to begin.

And once again, life intervened in a most unwanted and unexpected way. Outside, the sound of a truck rumbled swiftly up the driveway and came to a halt in front of the ranch house. The motor was cut. A telltale silence fell.

Mac lifted a brow. "Expecting someone?"

"No, of course not." Erin rushed to the window to see who it was. She peered out the blinds to see who was getting out of the vehicle, then groaned. "Talk about bad timing!" She shoved her hands through her hair, restoring order to the mussed strands. "What is *he* doing here?"

Chapter Fifteen

"What took you so long to answer the door?" G.W. asked Erin five minutes later.

"I was getting ready to go to work." *Or I would have been soon, anyway.*

He brushed past her with a disgruntled look. "Yeah, well, we need to talk, so it's a good thing the kids aren't here."

Erin agreed about that. The last thing their boys needed was to see them argue. Acutely aware that Mac was still upstairs, Erin led the way toward the kitchen.

"Why did you have Travis Anderson send your response to Horizon Oil? Why didn't you go through me?" G.W. appeared embarrassed.

Erin poured her ex a cup of coffee. She handed it to him the way he liked it—black. "I thought it would be easier."

"For whom?" he asked angrily.

"Laramie County isn't your territory anymore, G.W. It hasn't been since you requested a transfer after Angelica died." Erin poured herself a glass of water from the pitcher in the fridge. She sat down at the kitchen table. "Horizon Oil sent you to talk to me about signing over the mineral rights only because they thought you would have some influence over me."

G.W. sat down, too. "So?"

Erin gave him a level look. "So it was unfair of them to put you in that position, and really unfair of you to do the same to me."

He quaffed half his coffee in one long gulp. "Is that why you turned Horizon Oil down flat? Because you resented the use of our personal connection?" He rushed on. "Darn it all, Erin, I am trying to do you a favor here!" He flattened his palms on the tabletop. "The money you'd get from oil would allow you to make a fresh start elsewhere."

That again? "I don't want to make a fresh start."

He shook his head in condemnation. "You and the kids are never going to get over Angelica's death the way I have, unless you all physically move on."

Erin thought about Mac's present to her, the fact that he understood her need to not only never let go of the memories of her daughter, but to hold on to them with all her heart and soul for the rest of her life. Wearily, she told G.W., "We've been over this. I don't want to move on."

Her ex shook his head, turned away. And there, right where she'd left them on the kitchen table, were the various proposals Mac had given her. G.W. eyed the maps and diagrams bearing the North Wind Energy logo. "I gather you are still considering Wheeler's proposal."

Was she? In truth, there was only one question she wanted Mac to ask her, and he hadn't.

"I haven't said yes to anything yet, if that's what you're wondering."

"If he has anything to say about it," G.W.'s tone turned ugly, "you will."

Erin shifted into battle mode, too. "What's that supposed to mean?"

"Wake up, Erin. You accuse me, but Wheeler's using

his personal connection with you, too. Why do you think he moved in here with his little girl, who just coincidentally happens to be the same age our daughter would be right now, had she lived? Why do you think he's working so hard to ingratiate himself into your life? Because he knows getting on your good side is key to getting what he wants—the Triple Canyon."

Feeling as if she'd just had the wind knocked out of her, Erin drew in a shaky breath. "Mac's not like that."

"Oh, yeah?" G.W. pushed his chair back so hard and fast it scraped the floor. "Well, he seems pretty determined to me."

Without warning, Mac loomed in the doorway. Erin didn't know whether to be relieved that he had shown up to protect and defend her against her ex-husband, or sorry that he had just given G.W. more fuel in his argument about unfair business practices.

She knew full well what G.W. would say if he realized she had slept with Mac. That he had bedded her only to get her land.

G.W.'s surprised expression turned to one of contempt.

Mac walked over to pour himself a cup of coffee. The decanter was nearly empty, so he only got half a mug. "Everything okay here?" he asked casually. He turned to look at G.W. "I thought I heard arguing."

Erin swallowed and quietly pushed back her chair. She stood, too, conveniently positioned between both men. "G.W. was just leaving," she stated in a voice that brooked no discussion.

Her ex looked at Mac. "You hurt her. You hurt my family. You'll answer to me." He turned to Erin. "You've got some mighty big decisions to make here. Be sure, when you finally make them, that they are what you—and not what anyone else—wants."

He slammed his hat on his head and stalked out. The front door slammed behind him.

Half of Erin wanted to sink to the floor in a heap of tears. The other half had gone numb again. She swallowed and cleared away the coffee cups, dumping remnants in the sink. Made sure the warmer was off. "How much of that did you hear?" she asked, still not looking at him.

Mac folded his arms, clearly not pleased about what had gone down, or the fact that Erin had insisted he wait upstairs while she dealt with her ex.

"Enough to get the gist of it," Mac related. "He's wrong about me. I'm not using you or our relationship to sway you."

Erin gave a little smile. "I know that."

"And yet…" His eyes hadn't left hers.

She inhaled. "G.W. is right. I've got decisions to make that are going to impact my entire family for the rest of our lives. I need to make them alone, without undue influence—intentional or otherwise—from anyone."

Mac's eyes narrowed. "An hour ago you wanted to talk to me about all this."

An hour ago she had been looking for him to help her find a solution. She realized now that was unfair. She lifted a hand before he could come any closer.

"We're not a couple, Mac—in anything but a very temporary sense." If they had been, he would have told her he loved her, too, instead of delaying that conversation for much later. After the county commissioners' vote.

He opened his mouth, as if about to challenge that declaration.

Knowing her heart would break if he said anything now, Erin rushed on, making no effort to hide her aggravation. "The point is, this is all getting way too complicated. In a few weeks, you and Heather are headed back to Philadelphia to your life there. The boys and I will still be here—"

Mac interrupted her. "You know one way or another the wind farm is going to happen."

Erin nodded. That much had been clear after the bus trip to the Panhandle. The community was really on board. The county commissioners would follow.

"I don't care where it's set up," he told her.

Erin got that, too.

"And then you're going to leave," she said, swallowing a lump in her throat.

His eyes softened, as did his voice. He took her hand. "You could come with us. Run Monroe's from a distance. Set up a boot-making shop there."

She pulled away in a panic. "Now who's talking crazy?" This was all too much, too soon, too fast.

He remained where he was, but kept up the lobbying in a smooth-as-silk tone. "If we can adapt to Texas, who says you can't adapt to Pennsylvania?"

"Please, Mac." Erin felt a silly little flutter deep in her belly, the kind that always preceded their lovemaking. She drew a shaky breath. "Don't say any more."

He exhaled in obvious regret. "I know it's too early for us to have this conversation. It's why I didn't want to have it."

"And you were right," she agreed. She tucked her arms around her, reining her body in as tightly as her emotions. "We have our own lives, our own jobs and responsibilities. To that end, we have to put ourselves and our own families first."

Their eyes locked. "This sounds familiar."

Erin recalled what Mac had told her about Cassandra not consulting him on anything. About him being on the outside of every important decision. "This isn't the same as when you were married, Mac."

His jaw clenched. "It sure feels that way."

"I'm just asking for a few days to craft my own solution to the problem."

One that would leave her heart and soul intact.

He leaned forward intently. "I think we should craft one together."

Erin shook her head. "I can't do that, not without worrying about what you want, and giving short shrift to what I want."

He let his arms fall to his sides. "You're selling us short."

"I'm being honest."

Defeat glimmered in his blue eyes. "If the answer is no, just say no."

Feeling cornered, Erin blinked away her tears. "I can't do that, because I'm not sure it is no. And I'm not sure it's yes, either. I still just don't know!"

A skeptical silence fell. "Then what do you want?" he said after a moment.

Still wishing she could throw herself in his arms and make love to him until the whole world fell away, she met his gaze with raw honesty. "I want to stop feeling so pressured. By the community members who want lower utility bills, by the rural residents who want constant electricity, and by my family who want to be free, but who might one day really lament not having this ranch to call home."

She cleared her throat. "And most importantly, I don't want to be pressured by you. We both know you want to make the best deal possible for North Wind Energy so you can present the whole idea to the county commissioners for a vote, two days from now."

He rubbed his jaw, considering. Then leaned back against the counter, understanding her as much as he always had. "That is a lot of pressure," he said at last.

"Yes. It is," Erin replied emotionally, her knees sagging in relief that they'd gotten this far in their admittedly inefficient communications. "Thank you."

Still keeping his distance, he studied her. "So what do you need from me—if not answers to any more questions?"

Erin drew a deep breath, very much aware she could be laying down the deal breaker for their personal relationship. "I need you to accept that there is no more 'us' until all of this is over, Mac," she said seriously. "And that you find a way to make peace with whatever the final outcome ends up being."

"I CAN'T BELIEVE YOU'RE letting this deal go after all the work you've put in," Louise told Mac over the phone Thursday afternoon.

He pulled on the custom leather boots Erin had left for him. Buffed to a sheen, they were unbelievably comfortable and spiffy looking. "That's not what is happening here."

"Then suppose you explain why you haven't gotten everyone on board just two hours before the county commissioners meeting. Especially Erin Monroe."

"She asked me to give her space to make the decision. So I have." And it had been hard as hell doing so, when he knew she was running all over the county, talking to everyone but him about what she should do.

"Since when has that stopped you? Mac, you're one of the best executives North Wind Energy has! You never let anyone or anything get in the way of success. You do what you have to do to seal the deal."

That was him, all right. At least before he had arrived in Laramie County and met the good-hearted people here. Suddenly, it was about more than the units sold or the profits tallied. It was about actual human beings. Their needs, wishes, dreams.

Right now it was about Erin.

And *her* needs and wishes and dreams.

No doubt about it, he was off his game, professionally.

Personally, he'd never been closer to getting everything he ever wanted. That is, before Erin's ex-husband had burst in with the accusations that had brought her up short.

"Need I remind you that in order to become head of a regional sales office, you first have to make the deal in Laramie County?"

That had been the plan, Mac thought. "I'm not giving up on that," he said. No matter what, he knew where Heather and he belonged.

"And there's nothing you can do to convince Erin Monroe to sign on the dotted line?"

"Using unfair influence is not my style." He sighed. "Besides, that kind of pressure never works in the long run. Regrets set in, recriminations follow, then anger. Sometimes lawsuits."

Louise saw his point. "We don't need any ugliness down there. Not when we're trying to establish a real presence in the Texas wind energy scene."

"My thoughts exactly."

"So what is going to happen at the county commissioners meeting this evening?" she pressed.

"I was notified this morning I'm the thirty-sixth speaker on the agenda."

Louise made a sound that was half laugh, half moan. "Will they even get to you?"

Maybe sometime after midnight, when most of the residents had given up and gone home, Mac thought. "Depends on how long-winded they are."

His boss paused. "Is this a concerted effort to stop North Wind Energy?"

"I have no clue." All Mac knew for sure was that the first speaker on the agenda this evening was Erin. She'd be followed by attorney Travis Anderson and another lawyer. And then a whole host of other ranchers, including the Briscoes and the Armstrongs.

Once again, he was the odd man out in a sea of fiercely independent, kick-butt Texans. And he couldn't help but think he had Erin to thank for it.

His sense of exclusion and betrayal increased tenfold when he got to the community center, where the meeting was being held. The county commissioners sat behind a table on the stage. Five hundred local citizens filled the folding chairs set out on the floor. Local news camera crews were set up in the corners of the room. Sammy, Stevie and Heather were back at the ranch, in the care of a sitter, while Erin and her siblings gathered with their family attorneys in an area near the podium.

Mac greeted a few of the people he knew, then took a seat in the back, folder in hand. The Boy Scouts came in, carrying the county, state and American flags. The minister said a blessing, and the meeting was called to order.

Erin was introduced, and she walked to the microphone.

In a denim skirt, fancy red boots, T-shirt and embroidered cotton vest, her curly blond hair loose and flowing over her shoulders, she had never looked prettier. Or more at ease.

"Hello, everyone." She flashed the grin that always got him straight in the heart. "I know we're all frustrated with the shortage of electric power in the county, and we've all been looking for a solution. With the help of a few experts in the field, I think I may have finally located one."

Good to know, Mac thought resentfully. Now if only she'd told him first what it was!

"We started out talking about putting all the wind turbines on one property, my family's ranch. And while I see the logic behind that, because we aren't currently using the Triple Canyon for agricultural purposes," Erin continued seriously, "I'm no more willing to give up my family heritage to a wind farm than anyone else here. So Mac Wheeler—a very nice guy you've all met..." Erin searched the crowd until she saw him and smiled intimately.

Everyone turned to look at him, as if wondering why he was the odd man out if he and Erin were on such friendly terms.

Good question, Mac thought irritably.

He'd tried to be supportive. Gentlemanly. Suddenly, all he felt like was a wuss. And a pitied one at that!

Taking a deep breath, Erin continued, "When Mac started talking to some other ranchers to see if we couldn't share the wealth—so to speak—again, that was also met with mixed results, for the very same reason. Everyone wants to help out in theory, but when it comes to putting all those turbines on one property, people start to hesitate."

A murmur of assent rolled through the room.

"The county could of course exercise eminent domain and commandeer the property needed," Erin said, turning to look at the commissioners, "but no one wants to see that happen."

The crowd murmured in agreement.

Erin continued with a smile that confirmed she was the natural leader Mac had always deemed her to be. "So that started me thinking about who has been most affected by these rolling blackouts, and it's all the far-flung ranchers and rural residents. People who have land to spare, and who might agree to have a couple of hundred-foot towers on their property if those towers provided the electricity to run their ranches."

Mac began to see where this was going. Intrigued, he sat forward in his chair.

"So I looked into that and found out—just as Mac Wheeler once told me—that the towers currently available to individual users are generally much smaller and only make enough power to run a couple of appliances, at best." Erin sobered. "The ones that could run an entire ranch are so prohibitively expensive the individual ranchers would be hard-pressed to afford them. The county, on the other hand, already has money budgeted for the towers. So…" Erin paused to look the audience in the eye. "If we were to work out a deal between the landowners and the county, we just might have a solution that provides power and scattered towers across the entire county—"

"It's a good idea," a county commissioner interrupted, "but connecting all those towers to the power plant would increase the cost substantially."

And they weren't going to go for that, Mac knew.

He stood and lifted a hand. "If I may…"

With a nod from the chairman, he was given the floor.

Mac walked up to the microphone and took his place next to Erin. "It might work if, rather than trying to connect them all to one main source and then fanning out power from there, we used the couple of towers on each ranch to power it and its neighbors, individually." Mac looked at Travis Anderson and the lawyer he'd brought with him, a wind energy expert. "Granted, it would be complicated to hash out and would require a lot of work on the legal end of things. But if the county owned and installed the towers—and the residents gave up the land required, for a nominal leasing fee per year, and then paid the county for the electricity they used—it just might work."

"What about the town itself?" another resident asked, when called upon. "Are Laramie businesses and residences going to have enough electricity without expanding the plant?"

The director of public utilities shook her head. "No. They won't. We still need to bump up the capacity substantially, to prevent future problems."

Erin looked at Mac. "I'd be willing to have a hundred fifty of the required towers on Monroe land, as long as the thousand acres around the house and barns, and one of the canyons—the bluffs where we have a picnic pavilion—"

The bluffs, Mac thought, where the two of them had made love, and later, shared family time with everyone else.

"—are left intact," Erin continued. "If all of those towers are connected to the power plant, as originally planned, it would be enough for everyone else."

The crowd cheered enthusiastically. The county commissioner chairing the meeting banged his gavel and grinned. "Ladies and gentlemen, it looks like we may have a solution!"

To the wind energy problem, yes, Mac thought.

The situation between him and Erin was a different matter altogether. It appeared they were now further apart than ever…and he had no clue how to tear down the walls she'd put up between them.

"CONGRATULATIONS, ERIN!" the county commissioners said.

"Job well done!" Marybeth Simmons declared.

Darcy hugged Erin. "We knew we could count on you!"

And so it went for the next hour. Every time she tried to make her way to Mac's side, she was intercepted again. By the time she had spoken to the last well-wisher, he was gone. "Maybe I'll catch up with him back at the ranch," she told Nicholas.

"I don't think so," her brother said. "I just talked to the twins. They said Mac picked up Heather a few minutes ago. He took his bags with him."

Erin's heart sank. "Where did he go?"

Nicholas shrugged. "He said something about having to go to Philadelphia. Heather wasn't too happy. She was crying because they had to leave so unexpectedly."

A fresh wave of panic set in. "Did he say when he would be back?" Erin asked.

Her brother shook his head. "He told the twins he didn't know." Nicholas paused. "Do you think he's mad at you?"

Erin huffed. "Why would he be angry with me?"

Walking up to join them, Gavin rolled his eyes. "Duh. You blindsided him with your proposal, sis. The dude recovered nicely, but I don't think there was anyone here tonight who didn't know you deliberately cut Mac out of the solution-seeking process." Gavin shook his head. "That had to be embarrassing. Especially given how sweet he used to be on you."

Nicholas agreed. In fact, both her brothers were acting as if she and Mac were now over. Kaput. And all because of her. "He knows why I had to do it that way," Erin protested. They'd had an agreement, which Mac had honored, despite his ambitions. A fact that had proved to her G.W. was wrong—Mac *did* care about her immensely.

Maybe he didn't love her.

But love wasn't everything.

She had been foolish to believe it was.

What counted was what she and Mac had together. Their friendship and their passion, and the genuine way they cared about each other and their kids. "Besides," Erin continued defensively, "we worked together in the end."

Gavin scoffed. "He saved his deal from going under, Erin. There's a difference between that and working together, which, by the way, you did not do."

Erin glared at her brothers. They were wrong to crush her hopes and dreams this way. She folded her arms. "I'm sure I'll hear from Mac soon."

But she didn't.

Not that night. Nor the next day. Or the day after that.

Erin thought about calling him, then decided not to.

Maybe Mac needed his space, to work out things on his end, just as she had. If that was the case, when he was ready to speak with her, he would call her.

They'd talk about things and work everything out.

She told herself that throughout the entire weekend, and she was still telling herself that Monday morning. She even believed it, until the petite, crisp-looking brunette walked into Monroe's Monday afternoon.

"Erin? I'm Louise Steyn." Mac's boss handed over her card. "Executive VP of Sales. North Wind Energy. I'll be handling the negotiations with you and your family from this point forward."

Erin blinked. "Mac agrees with this?" And if so, what did that *mean?*

Louise smiled. "He requested it. He thinks it will be better this way."

Erin fought back tears. "So he's not coming back?" *Not ever?*

"On the contrary. He's busy setting up office space in the new professional building down the street from the community center."

Stunned, heartbroken, Erin could only stare. "He's going to be working here?" *And he didn't tell me?*

What did that intimate? Did she even want to know?

Louise studied Erin. "You can get any further details on that subject from him. What you and I should discuss are the contract terms. Is there a place we can talk privately?"

Reluctantly, Erin turned her attention to business. To her relief, Louise was as fair and considerate as Mac had been. Erin confirmed her family's agreement and directed Louise to Travis Anderson to complete the contract.

Finished, Erin went to find Mac. He was in his office, unpacking. He looked incredibly handsome, as expected. And incredibly reserved, which was not. A plaque already on the door said:

North Wind Energy Texas Headquarters
Mac Wheeler, Regional Vice President,
Marketing and Sales

Erin stared, the numbness she'd felt for days fading. In its place was a raw devastation. Somehow, she found her voice and her smile. "Did you get a promotion?" she asked, surprised at how tentative her voice could sound.

He kept working. "Yes."

Erin swallowed and moved past the open portal. "Congratulations."

He flashed his most impersonal smile. "Thank you."

The silence continued.

Obviously, he wasn't going to make this easy on her. The question was, would he let her back in at all? Her heart pounding, Erin pointed to the sign. "Does this mean you're back permanently?"

He nodded.

"Where's Heather?"

"Her Montessori school."

Erin edged closer. When she neared, she saw the circles beneath his eyes, which meant he had been sleeping as poorly as she. "Is she doing all right?"

Mac ripped open another box. "She's a lot better, now that we're back in Laramie." He frowned. "She probably won't be all that happy about staying at the Laramie Inn, or about the house hunting we're going to be doing this afternoon, though."

Erin moved closer still. She inhaled the brisk masculine fragrance of his aftershave lotion. "You don't want to stay at the ranch with us anymore?"

He turned a level look her way. "I don't think that's wise. Do you?"

No doubt about it, the barrier around her heart was totally gone. She could feel the pain, knew she was losing him. "I understand why you're upset with me."

Mac moved around to sit on the edge of his desk. "Do you?" he challenged.

Erin nodded, ready to grovel, if that's what it took. "I blindsided you at the meeting. I should have told you my plan."

Mac inclined his head, his emotional barriers still intact. "Why didn't you?"

Erin suddenly knew what it felt like to come up against a brick wall. She spread her hands helplessly. "I wasn't sure you'd agree, or even think it was possible. And I didn't want to argue with you about it when I knew in my gut that my idea would work."

And it had.

Mac was near enough to pull her into his arms. Instead, he sat there, hands resting idly on his spread thighs, eyes locked on her face. "And that's the only reason you shut me out?" he queried, even more softly.

She knew she had hit a nerve with him. She'd had plenty of time to think about it, too. She shook her head, suddenly on the verge of tears. "That's not the only reason," she said thickly.

He waited, steady as always.

"I was afraid."

"Of what?" He continued to listen, and suddenly she felt a spark of hope.

The tears came faster. "Of loving you with all my heart and you not loving me back. I was already depending on you so much. I knew I couldn't bear it if I fell even deeper in love with you and you still ended up moving back to Philadelphia."

Suddenly, she was on his lap, her bottom on his rock-hard thigh. He wrapped his arms around her, held tight, and pressed a kiss on the top of her head. "So you pushed me away instead."

"Not consciously. But, yes. I did. As a means of self-preservation."

"And now?" he asked, his own voice rusty.

"Now I miss you. I miss Heather. I miss the family we made. And I want it back." *Even if it means you never love me the way I love you.* "I want us to be a team," she told him fiercely.

"I want us to be a team, too." He wiped away her tears with his fingertips. "But first, I want us to be a couple. I want to share everything with you, Erin, good and bad. I want to know I can count on you, and I want you to know you can count on me. And I want to do all this because I love you and I have for a good long while."

Love! He'd actually said it? He loved her? Relief mixed with the joy spiraling through her. "Then why didn't you tell me that the day I confessed how I felt?"

It was Mac's turn to confess. "I told myself it was because I didn't want to put undue pressure on you or in any way muddle the business deal."

Her hands trembling, Erin prodded, "And now you know…"

He ran a hand down her spine. "That I was afraid, too. Of putting my heart on the line, making another mistake, finding myself in another relationship where I was shut out of every important decision."

Guilty as charged. "I'm not going to do that, Mac. Not ever again."

Satisfaction gleamed in his blue eyes. "That's good to hear."

Erin splayed her hands across his chest, reveling in the strong, steady beat of his heart beneath her palms. She looked deep into his eyes. "But you have to do something for me, too. If you need something and you aren't getting it, you have to let me know."

He smiled wickedly. "Like this?" He bent his head to deliver a steamy kiss.

Erin returned it with all her heart and soul. "Just like that," she whispered, kissing him back with building passion.

Finally, he lifted his head. Something sweet and intense passed between them. "Damn, but I've missed you, Erin," he murmured.

Her heart brimmed with happiness. "I've missed you, too, Mac."

He threaded his hands through her hair, his gaze as sincere as it was tender. "I don't want to waste any more time. I want to be with you. I want to make a commitment that will honor what we have and do our family proud. So marry me, Erin."

Was there ever any question? When she loved him so very much? "Yes, Mac." Erin wreathed her arms about his neck. "Yes!"

Epilogue

Six months later...

An autumn breeze blew across the back porch as Mac and Erin snuggled in the swing, watching Heather, Sammy and Stevie play with their new puppy in the backyard.

Homework and dinner awaited. And then one final play session with the puppy.

But right now, the two of them had a very important decision to make. Erin handed the color wheel to Mac. "You have to tell me what you like."

"I think you know what I like." He waggled his brows at her suggestively.

Erin laughed and nestled closer into the crook of his arm, contentment flowing through her. "You're right. I do."

Mac knew what she liked, too. So their lovemaking had taken on more depth, pleasure and meaning.

"But we're talking about our bedroom here," Erin continued determinedly. "And I need to know what color you'd like the decor to be."

Mac's brow furrowed. "What's wrong with the way it is now?"

Erin rolled her eyes. "Besides it being all pink and white, you mean?" And decidedly not masculine!

Mac shrugged affably. "Heather likes it."

Erin looked down her nose at him. "Heather isn't a grown man. And she doesn't reside in the master suite. Tell me the truth, Mac," she prompted seriously. "You'd rather have a more gender neutral decor."

He bent and kissed her forehead. "I don't care what color the walls and bedspread are as long as I get to hold you in my arms every night." He tightened his grip protectively and kissed her again. "And that's already happening."

"I don't deny that's the most special part of my day, either," Erin said. They'd been married three months now. And Mac had been home with her and the kids every night. What traveling he did happened during the day.

Nights, he had declared, were for his family.

The company had agreed.

And now his meetings with his boss in the Philadelphia headquarters were via videoconference, from his Laramie office.

Erin persisted, "But I want it to be a space we can both enjoy, in a color you would have picked out even if you weren't married to me." She pressed the wheel into his hands and fanned it out so all the colors were visible.

Mac glanced down. Within seconds, he had selected a masculine blue-gray that Erin liked, too.

"See?" she said happily. "That wasn't so hard, was it?"

He tucked a strand of hair behind her ear. "Not at all. Just don't ask me to look at any fabric."

Erin chuckled, knowing there were limits even for him. "I won't." She figured a nice paisley or plaid would do. "Besides," she continued, working up to the real subject here, "it's not like we're all done with pink."

Mac shifted, so they were even more intimately ensconced on the swing. "Heather decided what she wanted her new room to be?"

Erin nodded.

Since her twin sisters had graduated from nursing school and moved on, to big city hospital jobs and apartments in Dallas and Houston, and Gavin had moved out, too, buying a town house close to the Laramie hospital, the ranch had quieted substantially.

Now it was just her and Mac and their kids, and her brother Nicholas. "Heather's going to move into Bess's old room. And of course, paint it her favorite colors, fuchsia and pale pink."

Mac grinned. "So Angelica's old room..." with the trundle bed, where he and Heather had first bunked "...will soon be a guestroom once again."

"Mmm." Erin wrinkled her nose, happiness bubbling up inside her. "Not necessarily."

Mac noticed the deliberate mystery in her tone, and gazed at her.

"It's so close to the master bedroom. I think it would be a perfect nursery," Erin said quietly.

He blinked as the wonder of her words sunk in. "You're..."

"Going to have our baby in approximately seven months," Erin choked out hoarsely.

"That's incredible." A great big smile spread across his face, and he bent to bestow a tender kiss on her lips.

Happiness flowed through Erin that their efforts to make a baby together had been so successful, so quickly. "I saw my obstetrician today. She said everything looks good."

Mac nodded in relief. "Do you think it's going to be a girl or a boy?" he asked eventually.

Erin spread her hands. "No clue. I guess we're going to have to wait to find out."

And find out they did, seven months later, when twin girls were born.

"Not fair," Sammy and Stevie declared when they heard there were now three girls in the family and only two boys.

Mac and Erin laughed at the good-humored complaint.

Mac wrapped his two sons in his arms, while the girls in the family got better acquainted.

He bent down and said, with a conspiratorial wink, "Just give your mom and me a little time, fellas, and we'll see what we can do about evening up the score."

And two years later, when their son was born, they did just that.

* * * * *

Watch for Cathy Gillen Thacker's brand-new series McCABE HOMECOMING, *launching in May 2013, only from Harlequin American Romance!*

COMING NEXT MONTH
from Harlequin® American Romance®

AVAILABLE MARCH 5, 2013

#1441 COWBOY FOR KEEPS

Mustang Valley

Cathy McDavid

Conner Durham can't believe his luck—Dallas Sorrenson is finally single and free to date. Then he learns she's pregnant...and the father is the man who stole Conner's job.

#1442 BETTING ON TEXAS

Amanda Renee

City girl Miranda Archer buys a ranch in Texas, hoping to start over. But she has apparently stolen it from Jesse Langtry—a cowboy who's rugged, gorgeous and madder than hell at her!

#1443 THE BABY JACKPOT

Safe Harbor Medical

Jacqueline Diamond

After an unexpected night with sexy surgeon Cole Rattigan, nurse Stacy Layne discovers she's pregnant. But her recent donation of eggs to a childless couple means her hormones have gone wild. Result: she's carrying triplets!

#1444 A NANNY FOR THE COWBOY

Fatherhood

Roxann Delaney

Luke Walker desperately needs a nanny for his young son. Hayley Brooks needs a job. It's a perfect match—in more ways than one!

Welcome back to MUSTANG VALLEY,
and Cathy McDavid's final book in this series.
Conner Durham has gone from flashy executive to simple cowboy seemingly overnight. At least Dallas Sorrenson has appeared back in his life—and she's apparently single!

The laughter, light and musical, struck a too-familiar chord. His steps faltered, and then stopped altogether. It couldn't be her! He must be mistaken.

Conner's hands involuntarily clenched. Gavin wouldn't blindside him like this. He'd assured Conner weeks ago that Dallas Sorrenson had declined their request to work on the book about Prince due to a schedule conflict. Her wedding, Conner had assumed.

And, yet, there was no mistaking that laughter, which drifted again through the closed office door.

With an arm that suddenly weighed a hundred pounds, he grasped the knob, pushed the door open and entered the office.

Dallas turned immediately and greeted him with a huge smile. The kind of bright, sexy smile that had most men—Conner included—angling for the chance to get near her.

Except, she was married, or soon to be married. He couldn't remember the date.

And her husband, or husband-to-be, was Conner's former coworker and pal. The man whose life remained perfect while Conner's took a nosedive.

"It's so good to see you again!" Dallas came toward him.

He reached out his hand to shake hers. "Hey, Dallas."

With an easy grace, she ignored his hand and wound her arms loosely around his neck for a friendly hug. Against

HAREXP0313

his better judgment, Conner folded her in his embrace and drew her close. She smelled like spring flowers and felt like every man's fantasy. Then again, she always had.

"How have you been?"

Rather than state the obvious, that he was still looking for a job and just managing to survive, he answered, "Fine. How 'bout yourself?"

"Great."

She looked as happy as she sounded. Married life obviously agreed with her. "And how is Richard?"

"Actually, I wouldn't know." An indefinable emotion flickered in her eyes. "As of two months ago, we're no longer engaged."

It took several seconds for her words to register; longer for their implication to sink in.

Dallas Sorrenson was not just single, she was available.

Look for COWBOY FOR KEEPS, coming this March 2013 only from Harlequin American Romance!

HAREXP0313